DARKWIELDER

SARAH ZIMM

This book is a work of fiction. Names, characters, places, and incidents are either the product of the author's imagination or are used fictitiously, and any resemblance to actual persons, living or dead, business establishments, events, or locales is entirely coincidental.

Copyright © 2024 by Sarah Zimm. All rights reserved. No part of this book may be reproduced, stored in a retrieval system, or transmitted in any form or by any means, electronic, mechanical, photocopying, recording, or otherwise, without written permission from the publisher or author.

Book design by Okay Creations and Sarah Zimm
Map design by Chaim Holtjer

Ebook ISBN 979-8-9878859-4-9
Paperback ISBN 979-8-9878859-9-4

Printed in the U.S.A.

First Edition Ebook January 2024
First Edition Print November 2024

Everdark Press

READER PRAISE FOR

DARKWIELDER

"Dark and moody and perfect for fans of Leigh Bardugo."
—@mylastromancenovel

"Instantly immerses you back into the captivating world of Magus in the most intriguing and delicious way."
—@bookwhispererem

"Heartbreaking."
—@need.new.reads

"With haunting prose and complex characters, this was a novella that left me starved for more."
—@aubreycsanders

"I am completely in love and fearing the possibility of him being revealed as a true villian."
—@fireheart_13_

Books by Sarah Zimm

The Whispers of Dust and Darkness Series
Every Dark Shadow
Darkwielder (a novella)
Every Thread of Light

Series Reading Order
Darkwielder is a mid-series villain prequel that builds on the intricate world and characters introduced in book one. For the best reading experience, enjoy after *Every Dark Shadow*.

Content Warnings
For a full list, visit authorsarahzimm.com.

*For those made to feel they have to hide.
They are the monsters, not you.*

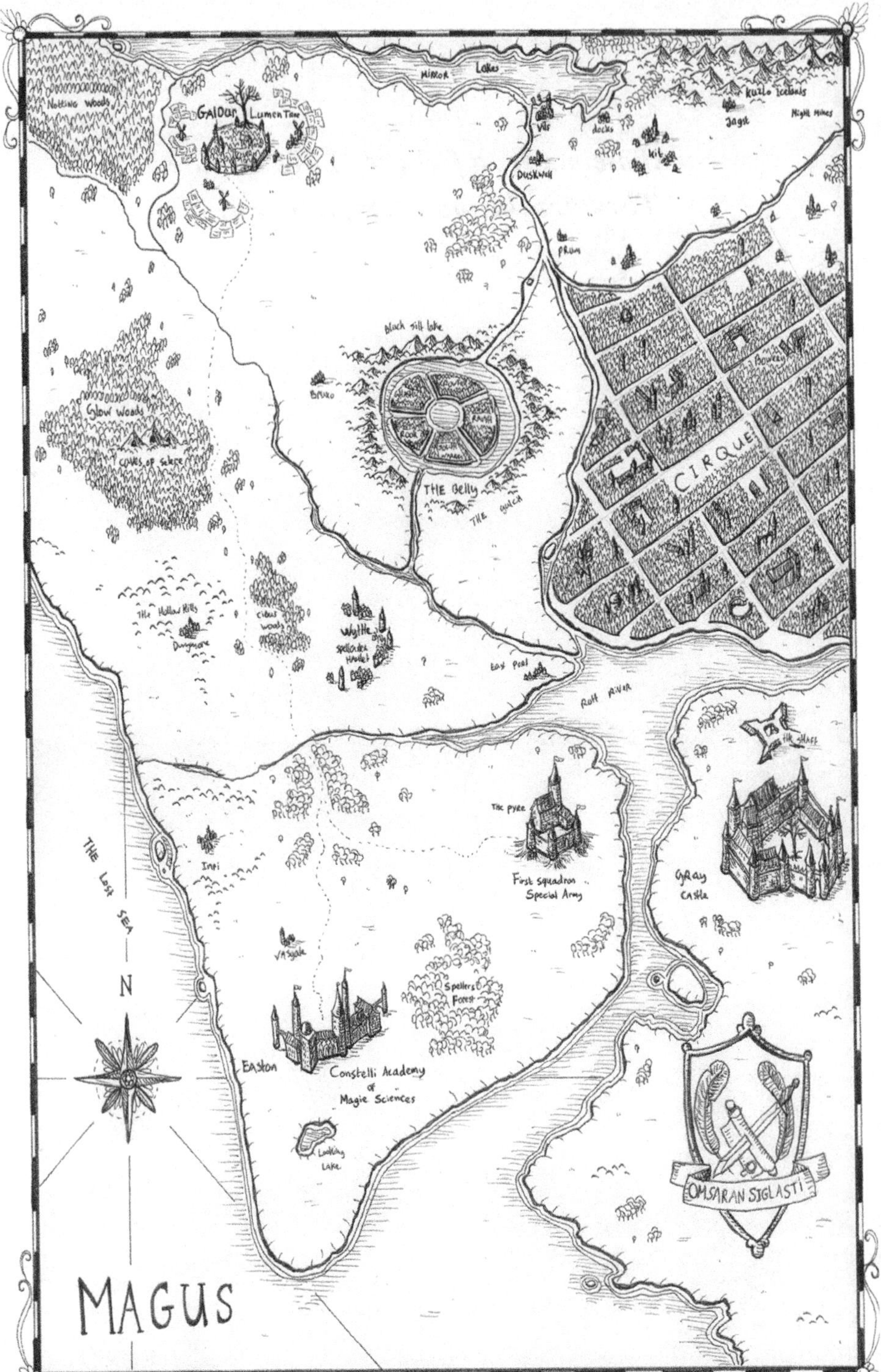

ORDER OF THE MAGIES

THE SPECIAL ARMY:
The King's Elite Magical Army
KNIGHT CAPTAIN
SERGE
LIEUTEN
PRIVFIR
PRIV

THE CONSTELLI
Academy of Magie Sciences
HEADMASTER
SAGES
APPRENTICES
STUDENTS

WITCHISTS
Guild of Spellers
SHADOWCASTERS
SPELLCASTERS
ANIMATERS

MATTERISTS
Guild of Influencers
BENDERS OF FLAME | AIR | WATER
ENCHANTERS

MORPHISTS
Guild of Transformers
SHIFTERS
FABRICATERS

Chapter 1
Edge of Death
Spellcaster Hamlet, Wythe
Present Day

"*Someday they will call you king.*"

The words ring in the Darkwielder's mind from long ago. But here, in this pit, there is excruciating pain.

Foggy with it, he lurches up from where he's been lying in a fissure in the earth, groping in the smoke, dust, and dirt as debris pounds like rain, until he hits a wall of something hard and his body slides.

Gravity seems to swoop, knocking his head back.

It's a moment before he manages an eye open again and sees what he's narrowly missed—death at the bottom of this great crack in Magus's earth.

Above him somewhere roars sounds that are separate from the echoes in his mind.

It takes a moment more to remember the events that transpired this night in Wythe—the curing of the king's curse, the tremoring earth, the clash of armies, the fire and air belting across a broken dais. He remembers now, how he called out to Ophelia

Dannan before the ground split and something massive struck him from behind, sending him into this would-be grave.

As he remembers, defeat throbs through his head, his back, and an arm, and with a deep cough, the pain spiders into his lungs while his vision clouds red with his own blood.

He can see his boots, though, just skimming the edge of the dirt cliff where he's slid to his back.

He can see down into the gaping seam that stretches to vast depths.

He—the Darkwielder.

When he passed into Wythe from the Belly, he heard Jasper Salt speak that name to Ophelia Dannan. *The Darkwielder.* It's what they all call him—his enemies and his people. A name for his power. For a creature, not a person.

Something skids above him, sending a fresh assault of dirt crashing down.

"Am Kosost!"

He rolls his head toward the desperate voice calling through the smoke. His legs draw up, intending to stand, but the pain rears and he bites his lip to stifle a cry of anger, of defeat.

He can't move. He's bleeding—maybe inside—and not foolish enough to think immortal power means he cannot die.

In the thick air, Jasper Salt's silhouette leans farther over the edge, fifty feet up where Wythe is crumbling.

But where is she?

He sees only his proxy, the leader of the Special Army, though his splitting vision makes Jasper's face look like two. Flames lap around his envoy in the smoky air that's raining remnants of battle down on the Darkwielder. It's ash and...snow. One curse lifted, another plague bestowed by the settling triple moons.

Winter.

"I'm coming!" Jasper's voice whips down, and in it the Darkwielder can hear his proxy's fears, begging, *We are so close. Don't let it end now.* "Don't move!"

He doesn't, but even on his back, without seeing the damage, he feels what's been lost: the upper hand and Ophelia Dannan.

He manages to raise a heavy hand to his head where it throbs. It comes away wet, dark with blood that's been spilling into his eyes.

"You could probably heal yourself, if you had to," a voice purrs from his past, one that makes his chest tighten, and he instantly feels for his power, for his...

"Where?"—he coughs—"Where is..."

The Dark Shadow.

He felt the singe, soul deep, when Ophelia Dannan stripped the Spellcaster hamlet of the darkness. He aches for it with equal measures of longing and vengeance, as he did in all the quiet waiting years in the Belly.

Above, a few soldiers are crouching beside Jasper, pointing, trying to find a path to pick their way down into the seam to salvage him.

Can there be salvaging this time?

What of the king?

What of Ophelia Dannan?

He closes his eyes.

It should take less than a breath to feel his power. Instead, it takes the last of his strength. It's far away, beating like a faint pulse.

His hollow bones call out to it, seeking the cold, vast, dark companion so wholly of him now. He seeks Ophelia, too, calling and calling until his body vibrates with a pain that splits from his head down his spine, urging him to find a true healer.

Find a healer or...

His gaze drifts to the sky, beyond Jasper Salt, beyond Wythe burning, as defeat carries his thoughts to the past that set all this in motion.

Chapter 2
The Invitation
Gray Castle, Cirque
Thirty-five Years Ago

H is shadows were lonely company.

At a writing desk timbered with red bounty wood, where a quill sat untouched and a crisp parchment blank, Kier flicked his wrist to make his shadows dance. It wasn't difficult. At his half-hearted command, they raced in thin ropes across the tutoring room, up a double staircase, past wall shelves filled with books, to a landing where a lamp burned in a chandelier near a single window.

Kier closed his fist, and the warm glow was swallowed by shadows. They were cold-blooded things—his shadows—and, like him, craved warmth.

Only the autumnal gloom out the rose window remained in the room, casting a pallor on Kier's face. He didn't need a mirror to know he looked pale. The ivory of piano keys, one of his attendants always dared to tease. The sun didn't look often on his face. Not many at Gray Castle did, for that matter.

He played with the thin coils, more out of boredom than for practice. When he freed two fingers from his fist, the glow of the lamp stole in frets across his desk. He let the light ebb and flow to ticks of the clock on the wall, as a beacon would flicker in a storm, and listened to the castle sounds.

A crackle of wood splintering in the hearth. Quiet servants in the halls. Shallow grunts and gallops of horses outside, timed to ringing orders of the Royal Army. Kier glanced at the clock—a notch shy of late afternoon. So, guards changing shifts.

Jeering shouts caught his ear. A brigade of voices that sounded his age.

His fingers unclenched instantly, and the desk bathed again in warm light. He was out of his seat and up the stairs, pushing tall in his polished boots and bearing against the unforgiving fabric of his coat—stiff as a tourniquet at the shoulders and neck—to see outside.

In the vast, mazing courtyard of stonework and shrubbery, royal guards stood at posts around the lawn. Beneath great walls and twisting spires, visitors were taking the air.

Kier's eyes flicked east. At the edge of the yard, beyond a blooming tree with bloodred leaves, just outside a massive gray tent taut with spikes, he counted six boys in all. Nearby, servants readied horses with saddles.

Kier scarcely rode, though he liked to watch the army train the animals and imagine himself at the reins. But these were not the warrior horses the Royal Army rode. They were lithesome, sure-footed steeds.

The boys were vocal, and their words carried through the open window in snatches. One made Kier's hand twitch.

Boarhound.

The formal hunt. Had it already been half a year? It could be hard to mark time in a world where seasons stretched years, when you had few people to measure it with.

Kier rarely spied young people on castle grounds aside from servants born or brought here. Mostly, it was high-borns from the capital of Cirque—Crats—and representatives from the seven regions who came on political business. But during hunts, boys from Cirque's upper crust who were nearing eighteen were invited from Bowery to hunt the boarhound.

Kier had seen the creatures in books. They looked small but, according to lore, were mean as devils. They bred well in forests where magic gathered thickly and fed fruit-heavy trees, which meant their numbers had to be thinned twice each year.

Watching the boys, he felt a twinge of excitement. Dogs ran around them. They laughed with such ease, patting one another's shoulders and swatting each other's hats in jest.

An echo of a reprimand came sternly in his mind, in his uncle's grand bellow. *"A boy like you does not need friends. You have something greater—a purpose."*

Still, Kier watched as a seventh boy went rushing from the courtyard to join the group.

The hunts began at twilight when the boarhound stirred. He was trying to imagine what it would be like to welcome the triple moons and pink-red dusk from the back of a mount, among friends, when the smack of a spellstaff against the door frame jerked Kier from the window, as if it'd grabbed him by the collar.

An old man robed in scarlet threads stood at the bottom of the stairs, the dark-gray mustache above his beard frowning at Kier.

The door snapped neatly shut behind Grimm Hermes as he entered. "Young Kier." The words were admonishing, and the room seemed swallowed up by the presence of this oldest living

Spellcaster, a man who'd been Kier's private tutor since he could speak.

"I was taking a small break from my work," Kier explained.

Grimm curved one hand over the knot of his staff and waved the other at him. "I could see your *work* from the courtyard as I approached. Do I need to remind you what your uncle would say?"

Kier sighed. "No." He hated how meek he sounded. He took the opposite staircase down, giving his tutor a view of his back and slouching shoulders, and sank into his desk chair. "He commands I stay in the shadows."

Grimm came slowly over, his staff punctuating each step on the hard marble. The tutor cast a knowing look toward the window, and Kier thought he saw a flicker of empathy.

He latched onto it. "I'm eighteen in a few days, and this is the last hunt before I'm to ascend next week. I was thinking perhaps it's worth asking him if—"

Grimm raised his staff, and the curtains rodded above the window slid shut. He lowered his salted brow. "Your uncle is many things. But have you ever known the king of Magus to change his mind or take risks where you're concerned?"

Kier picked up his quill and twirled it, then pressed the tip to his palm's meaty flesh. "I don't know what he thinks will happen." The tip of the quill pierced his skin, and blood spotted. Unbidden, a shadow licked from Kier's wrist, lashing at the quill.

Grimm peered at him. "You don't know what he thinks will happen? If the kingdom learns their king is raising a Magie nephew at the castle?"

Kier did know.

The king had feared it aloud plenty. His supporters might draw conclusions the king was wavering from his original cause—undoing the moral corruption and mortal suffering caused by Magie rulers. He might be ousted, or forced to take Kier's life in a demonstration of commitment to his platform.

Yes, Kier knew. But he was brooding.

Grimm came nearer, and the glow of the chandelier cast on his centuries-old features. "I tell you this not for *him* but you. It's growing more dangerous for the magic-born in this world, Kier."

Kier sat forward, elbows on his knees. "He could bring Magus together. He's half-Magie."

"Your uncle did not become king fifteen years ago by celebrating that half."

And yet, his uncle would raise a full-born Magie, Kier thought. That must mean he cared, in his way. He would acknowledge him publicly when the time was right.

For now, there were few who knew Kier was the king's relation, and fewer who knew he was Magie. Grimm did. Some trusted kingsguards, too. And Kier's personal attendants. As for anyone else at Gray Castle, they were told he was distant kin of some dead friend of the king. If they saw Kier and suspected anything more, they would never ask.

"Men become kings by choosing sides in this world," Grimm lectured. "Your uncle chose his long ago, and while we can't prevent the fire set to our kingdom, we can choose not to toss ourselves into the flames."

Kier frowned at the sage. "Why do you always teach in riddles?"

"To sharpen your mind. A time may come, young Kier, when you will have to ask yourself what course you'll set. If you'll walk the path of your ancestors or chart a better way."

Grimm's brow looked so serious, but Kier couldn't fathom what lesson he was meaning to impart. Granted, he was distracted, his gaze wandering up the stairs to the shut curtains.

It was suffocating, being invisible.

"Kier." Grimm came into his eyeline. "You ascend next week. You'll take your place in the king's new army and be able to live openly as Magie. Until then, it's safer this way. No more displays. Now finish your maps." Grimm knocked his staff at the edge of Kier's desk.

Safer this way. For Kier.

That's what his uncle—the king—had said when he told Kier of the new Special Army. It was at the same private dinner where he'd announced Grimm Hermes would be headmaster at the new academy. Grimm would leave Gray Castle next week, while Kier would be sent with a hundred other Magies from across the kingdom to train as soldiers. In four years' time, Kier himself would lead the new army for the king.

He wasn't sure what he felt more—pride at being chosen or nerves over what the job might entail. He'd heard all about what the Royal Army did—enforcing kingdom law, collecting taxes, handling dissent.

"What will the Special Army do?" he'd asked the king at their last dinner, after the young Royal Army commander Jory Dagon had broken in and informed the king of an incident—an attack on soldiers en route to the west by Magies protesting the king's rule.

"The army will make you safer," his uncle had assured.

Kier dipped his quill to the inkpot on his desk and drew the long Rott River on his parchment. For the next hour, he mapped villages from his lesson books by memory. The captain of the new Special Army would need to know them all. That's what the king had said.

"Because the Special Army will serve as protectors?" Kier had asked.

It was only after his uncle vaguely replied, "Of course," and dismissed him, that Kier realized his question hadn't been clear. He hadn't had the nerve to amend it, to clarify what exactly he was being tasked to protect.

He was still thinking of Grimm's riddles and the hunt an hour later as he walked a long arched hallway that led directly to the servant's wing.

The walls felt like eyes here, embellished with carved plaster designs and figures that gave the impression of creatures trying to claw their way out.

Grimm had instructed Kier, as always, not to dawdle returning to his chambers. The Spellcaster had a meeting to attend and couldn't walk him back, but he'd seemed sufficiently convinced Kier wouldn't do anything unwise after their talk. Had he ever, in all his childhood?

Kier paused at the alcove where a narrow staircase marched to chambers, letting two maids come down with baskets of linens to wash.

"Gretya. Marga." His voice was quiet, polite, as he nodded at each of them in turn.

The women moved in a rush, barely meeting his eyes.

Kier tried not to feel the sting.

They were Magies, as many servants were. He'd learned all their names. But with a few exceptions, most were wary of Kier Lestat, the boy who lived in back staircases and hidden passages, along with the library and other quiet places, who explored the halls and yard as a ghost might, when the castle slept. When they did see Kier in the light of day, they seemed to see the king over his shoulder, too. A king who told them to keep their distance. So they did.

"Cowards," he muttered as the servants disappeared. Then again, he was probably one, too.

The thought barely formed when light footsteps tread at his side.

He stepped back as another servant approached the alcove, on her way up with folded linens that brought the smell of jasmine and wind.

She was golden and tall—nearly as tall as he—and didn't hurry past him but paused at the step where his foot hovered. He blinked quickly, then snapped his head in a nod. "Delphine."

"Master Kier." Her words were a breath, and his heart stuttered when she peeked at him through long lashes, holding his gaze a full second before a tiny smile pulled up her cupid bow mouth and she slipped past him.

Kier started up behind her. But after two-and-a-half steps and another word on his lips, a slew of loud, young voices rooted his feet in place. He watched the servant girl's braid swish at her back with the movement of her hips, and he thought one moment about *wise* decisions.

Biting his lip, he retreated downstairs, curiosity winning.

With haste, he edged down the hall, straightening the collar of his dark coat. The king didn't allow him to wear gray like others at court, but black felt more like him, anyway. Dark clothes for the boy who lived in shadows.

Around a corner, another barrel-ceilinged hall unfolded in front of him, splitting east to west. Kier had never spent time in this wing but knew there was a door that led to below-ground tunnels, connecting the castle to the prison. The east hall held extra rooms for visitors. And in between was a wide, curving staircase that led down to the guests' dining hall.

The voices carried again.

Kier knew before creeping to the landing that they belonged to the Crat boys come to hunt. Heading to dinner first, he waged. But they were out of sight swiftly, and he shook his head at himself. It wasn't like he could follow them.

Turning back, he stopped hard, faced with a boy whose hair was ablaze in red-orange strands. He was built wiry as a colt and already dressed in riding clothes. This was the one he'd seen rushing to join the group outside.

The boy tipped his head curiously at Kier with a smirk on his mouth, then to the stairs, and back. "Hello," he offered. "I haven't seen you around."

The boy's interest dropped to Kier's coat, to where his rolled maps were tucked. He approached until he was only a foot from Kier, who stepped a foot back. "Are you a guest here, too?"

Lie to him. "Of a sort," Kier answered carefully, keeping one hand tucked in his coat.

"You don't have the snobbish nose of a Bowery gent." The boy laughed lightly. "Which part of Cirque do you hail from?"

Kier glanced up the hall. It was empty. "I grew up close by."

"You should join us on the hunt then. We have extra steeds..." He waited, giving Kier an opening to supply his name.

Kier had many in his arsenal, thought up on nights he couldn't sleep, in case he ever met someone who asked or found himself in a part of the world that couldn't know who he really was. Lest it fall back on the king.

"Warrick." He'd read the name in a story about pirates, a pillager of wealthy ships who stole the king's treasures to sustain the poor.

Before Kier knew it, the boy extended a hand and took his, pumping it once. "Ahren."

Kier panicked, looking where he gripped his palm. Then quickly remembered this was a custom among mortals, when inviting friendship.

Ahren didn't know Kier was Magie.

"We have plenty of supplies. I can save a gun and a saddle for you." The boy looked around the empty halls. "If you'd like a few friends."

Kier was speechless at the invitation.

The boy stepped around him. "We leave at first moons. Don't be late." With a wave, he disappeared.

Watching him go, Kier felt a thrill of excitement rise.

It sunk just as quickly when movement caught his eye down the west hall. Gray robes. A crown glinting with seven spikes. His uncle, with hair so black it was nearly blue and a severe look permanently etched between combed brows, was coming from the direction of the prison doors.

Who he might be seeing at the prisons so close to dinner, when he had guests to entertain, Kier couldn't say.

Kier wasn't supposed to be here.

Judging by the tempo of his stride, the king had already seen him. It was too late to go, so Kier straightened his spine.

His uncle was a storm arriving before him, surrounded by his servants and personal guards, including Jory Dagon, who was only twenty but a beast of a man with a sword. He'd tried to train Kier, for months, but steel hadn't been Kier's strength.

"What are you doing here?" His uncle grasped his arm, leading him the way of the servants' wing. At the stairs, Kier tried to keep his chin up. He suspected the king smelled things in blood that others couldn't. Weakness and power.

Kier tried to find a balance—not too remorseful, not too bold. "I was hoping to thank you for the extra lessons with the Spellcaster, and see if there's anything else I might do to prepare myself for ascending next week. I know it's only a private ceremony, but..."

The king passed a look at Jory, nodding to his guards. They cleared a space around them, and the king motioned Kier to the stairs. He didn't touch his nephew as they climbed together. And it wasn't until they reached the landing he spoke again.

"I've decided your *Asenti* will include an audience. There hasn't been one in years. If it's to be a formal occurrence at the academy going forward, yours will set precedent."

Kier's surprise and hope swelled so fast, his shoe clipped a step and he nearly tripped.

A public coming out? The king would acknowledge him as kin before an audience?

But the king went on briskly. "My representatives are mortals. They have notions about your kind." *Our kind*, Kier thought. "They need to be shown what they're investing in and see it will be...controllable. We'll tell them you're from the north. It'll assuage them that barbaric region can be brought to heel and that, soon, we'll have full access to their mines."

"But it isn't true."

The king arched a stiff brow. "It'll give us time to sway the north's *volorost* and earn you some measure of respect."

Kier's mouth twitched and fell. "So it's political."

The king's court wanted the north's lucrative *migth*, metal that was spelled by the moons and worth more by the ounce than a carriage full of coin. But it wasn't as simple as sending his armies in to get it—the north had to *let* you in. From what Kier had overheard all his childhood, winged creatures patrolled the icelands from the air, guarding the mountains, the mines, and the people there.

So it seemed while Kier craved family, the king craved the last place Magies still had a foothold, and feigning a connection would allow Kier a place in the king's world. But not as his nephew.

"You don't plan to tell them I'm your kin."

Something passed in the king's eyes, leaving just as swiftly, as he finally replied, "It would be too much at once for them. Someday, when the time is right."

Kier felt no pride or nerves then. As they neared his chamber door, it was all he could do to reach for courage. If he was to become a symbol—a puppet, a pet—was it too much to ask for one night on his terms, out of the dark?

"Uncle. The boarhound hunt in the bounty wood tonight... I heard some of the boys and wondered—"

"Don't." The king held up a hand in warning. It shone with a gaudy silver ring. "One week, and you'll display yourself to the representatives and a *prüstrot*. The kingdom will be watching to see the power you wield is in service to this crown. You have far greater things that should be occupying your mind and ears than boarhound."

"But uncle—"

Out of nowhere, the king's hand flew up and pain exploded across Kier's cheek. He lowered his face instantly and had to cuff a hand at his wrist to stop his shadows from leaching.

The king's chest shook a sigh loose. After a moment, his palm came to rest on Kier's shoulder, and Kier looked up. He was surprised at the stitch of remorse—or wariness—in his uncle's brow.

The king didn't apologize. He squeezed Kier's shoulder, only just too hard, then let it go. "No more talk of hunts. And don't let me see you again in the west wing."

K ier's cheekbone throbbed as he shut his chamber door.

With quiet rage clenching his jaw, he let his rolled maps fall on the table that stretched a quarter of his room. His meal was already set at the end with a water pitcher. A feast for one of wild game in fruit sauce, venison pie, foraged mushrooms, and lemon cake.

He took a few long strides to it and swung his arm viciously, swiping the plate and sending the silver, the pitcher, and the platters to the marble floor in an angry heave.

A set of gasps made his head whip.

"Master Kier!" A woman rushed forward from where she'd been standing near his bed, smoothing out covers, with two other servants.

Bridgen's eyes were wide on him, on the mess. And her words—*Master Kier*—were chiding.

Bridgen was mortal and all business. In the time she'd been assigned as Kier's lead attendant, he wasn't sure he'd ever seen her smile. He wondered if that was by order of the king. But he was looking past Bridgen now to the servant girl with the golden braid, whose hazel eyes were mooned in surprise at him. A boy of eight hid behind her.

Kier blinked at them. Delphine and her brother.

"I'm sorry," he said quietly. "I didn't realize anyone was here." Kier stooped to pick up chards of broken things.

Bridgen clucked her cheek. "You're bleeding on the floor."

He was, he realized. He'd cut his hand, deeply enough he didn't feel it at first. As soon as he saw the blood, he swayed on his feet, and it began to sear.

Fetching a broom brush, Bridgen shooed him with it. "Into the wash room, young master. Go." She hardened a look at the other servants and called impatiently for the young boy to come help her clean.

Delphine's body was as rigid as a shield in front of the child. "He can't hear you," she reminded Bridgen. But they'd been assigned to Kier two years. He doubted Bridgen had forgotten.

Kier moved across the room and, with one hand, signed to the boy as he'd seen Delphine do—*R-h-o-d-i-n*—and gestured an apology.

Delphine nudged him, and the golden-locked boy smiled and scurried past Kier to take Bridgen's broom pan.

Delphine didn't move from her place near the wash room door.

When Kier passed through it into the wallpapered room laden with porcelain and crushed velvet, the door clicked shut behind him.

He barely turned before Delphine's hands were on his face, pulling his mouth to her full lips.

Warmth blanketed Kier, like shadows curling around lamplight.

He held his bleeding hand up, ignoring the wetness trailing down his sleeve. His other palm roamed to her back, pulling her close. He breathed in the scent of jasmine and wind that was tangled in her hair and fragrant on her skin.

Unrestrained and hurried, the kiss made his wounded hand, his uncle's rejection, the torturously long hours in the tutoring room, and his loneliness in the days between this—a stolen moment—easier to bear.

"Maybe I should be wounded more often." Kier smiled against her lips.

They were both breathless, and though he wanted to keep her there, her forehead to his—to savor the touch of someone who knew *what* and *who* he was—Delphine pulled out of his hold.

"Wounds are serious. Don't be stupid," she answered softly, though her smile betrayed her.

She motioned for him to sit on the dressing chair near the tub. It was a tufted seat Kier had curled into after baths as a child for lack of a mother's arms, for lack of anyone who might stay longer than to towel him dry.

"Servants are paid to do their job, not be his friend," he'd overheard the king tell Grimm once, a few years ago when Kier had sulked in his room all day, when he couldn't bear the quiet or Bridgen's not-talking anymore.

"A boy needs a friend," Grimm had insisted. "It's affecting his studies. At the least, consider giving him a hound."

"Hounds are loud and filthy."

"Then a servant, someone his own age. I'll choose them myself, one with something to lose, if it gives you assurances."

Delphine.

Obediently, Kier sat, his gaze fixed on her. He wondered, as always, what she saw in him that others didn't. He was built slender, for running and slipping easily through trees. He lacked color, and often humor. Then there were his shadows. What must she really think of them? To Kier's knowledge, there were no others here at the castle who could wield them.

Delphine knelt on the marble floor before Kier, letting her brown skirt billow behind her. "Let me see it."

He gave his hand freely, craving the feel of her silken fingers against his palm. It took his mind off the fact he was still bleeding.

She wore a cuff at her wrist with a single red jewel, nearly covered by her sleeves. She inspected his cut like a mortal surgeon might, unbothered she could see inside him.

Kier was struck by a sudden morbid fascination. Could she see his darkness in there, looming? Did it show in his blood? His bone?

He didn't check, or he'd have to admit to her he was squeamish. And she was someone who didn't look at Kier like he was strange or meek. Or the opposite—frightful enough to command an army of Magies. He was just a teenage boy.

"You could probably heal this yourself, if you had to," she said softly. "If you'd practice."

"It wouldn't be as pleasant."

Her blue-green eyes caught his. He knew why she was telling him this. Because he'd be leaving soon. Grimm had told him once that shadows could staunch wounds. He liked the idea, but...not the blood.

Blood was one of his first memories. It was probably impossible—probably only a remnant of his childhood imagination, or stories he'd overheard about what happened to other children—but Kier could picture himself as a small child, sitting in a pool of it.

Murmuring, Delphine pressed a hand over his wound. A tingle grew. A warm sensation. Then a brief tightening.

"How did you learn to heal so well?"

As soon as he asked, he realized what a stupid question it was.

She'd shown him the scars along the back of her arms from before she and Rhodin arrived at the castle with their father—a Magie so desperate to make a better life, he became obsessed with science and the idea of buying his way into court.

"He thinks with science he can replicate magic, that he can bottle its effects and it'll make things even between mortals and the magic-born," Delphine had explained.

Kier had felt sick. She'd meant effects like healing. Like what she could do. And though Delphine swore her father left her and Rhodin alone now that they all lived at the castle, Kier had begged his uncle to forbid the experiments.

The king had told Kier to focus on his studies.

"Wipe the pity off your face, Kier," Delphine said now. "Having to heal myself every night as a child made me stronger. It could make me valuable here someday."

Kier couldn't smooth his frown, though, even as she pulled her hand away and he saw the blood and his wound were gone. There wasn't even a scar.

She sat back. "I've never seen you so angry. What happened?"

Kier leaned forward, itching to cup her cheek. The invitation from Ahren, the Crat boy, came out in a rush.

"I want to go," he admitted. "I told the king as much—"

Her brows knitted. "You know better than to go against the king." Delphine scrambled to her feet and straightened her apron, glancing at his cheek.

He'd already forgotten about it, though it must still be red.

"You know what he could do to you. There are rumors among the servants, Kier."

He lightly took her wrist. "He won't hurt me. I'm part of his plan. And I think"—he saw his uncle's face in his mind, just after he'd struck him—"I think he cares for me, even if he won't admit it." He looked up at her, feeling raw. "It's just... He believes love makes us weak. Do you think he's right?"

Delphine swallowed. "You aren't supposed to ask a girl if she loves you round-about that way."

He smiled. "You've told me you love me."

"I've told you it doesn't matter that I do. You're leaving, and we're seventeen. In a year, I'll probably love some other handsome fool."

He knew she was lying. It'd been two years, and he'd never seen her so much as look at another. "Handsome?"

She shook her head at him in exasperation, but he rose his chin.

"Love doesn't care about distance, Delphine. I'll feel the same when I'm at the army."

"Or maybe you read too many stories."

He shrugged. "When I return for you someday, you'll see."

"You'll be too powerful and special to spare a glance at me then."

"Never. But I may be too powerful and special to go on a hunt. It's now or never, don't you think?"

He waited for her to agree, or to kiss him again. She didn't. She simply said, "Don't be stupid."

When Bridgen called through the door, Kier dropped his hand. "You're right," he said as he left the wash room. "Probably foolish."

But he would take his chances.

Chapter 3
Dark Are The Woods
Gray Castle, Cirque
Thirty-Five Years Ago

Stepping out from behind the last pillar in the courtyard, Kier fastened the buttons on the collar of his new coat.

The coat was gray.

He'd found it in the laundry, along with a hat, and planned to return it. He'd only have this one night before he'd once again wear black forever.

At the edge of Gray Castle, where the sky above was streaked with a final burst of pink, Crat boys were gathering at the large gray tent with flags on top.

Kier worked his way toward them.

Fortunately, the second hunt of the year wasn't the spectacle of the first. Neither the king nor his representatives attended. They preferred their politics and parties.

Kier had waited until the guests meandered to the ballroom, until he was certain the king had gone, too. He waited until all the halls were empty, then he'd dismissed his attendants early for the night.

Delphine—and Rhodin, who rarely left her side—had already been pulled to help with the party, and Bridgen, never the nurturing sort, had been easily convinced to leave him.

Approaching the tent, Kier saw it held only guards, off post, and some court visitors he assumed were avid hunters themselves. They mingled inside, drinking wine and feasting from plated dishes. Only two men sat outside, comfortable in a pair of plush chairs. He guessed they were overseeing things, but they paid little attention to the dogs howling or to the boys readying saddles and strapping guns and blades to belts.

Kier kept his head lowered, approaching slowly.

This was forbidden. Was he sure? What if a guard recognized him?

He stalled there in the shadow of the tent, near enough he could hear Ahren, the boy with the fiery hair, address the other boys, most of whom shifted on their feet and looked impatient.

"...he'll be here," Ahren said. "With eight, we could take a wider route. My brother got a boarhound near the northern trail along the One Sea last hunt. He says they prefer it at twilight to prey on nightbirds..."

"Child's play," a voice scoffed from the huddle. "We can do better than a single boarhound. A mother and her whole brood."

Kier's face pinched at the idea.

Weak, he chided himself. If he was going to hunt—let alone lead an army someday—he had to stomach the stuff men did.

The owner of the gritty voice had their back to Kier, but he could see a robust frame, larger than his own, and a lick of dark hair sticking out beneath a rounded hat, as they twisted to belt a gun at their waist.

It was only when they turned to the side Kier realized they were female.

She folded her arms at Ahren. "Well? I don't see this eighth you've promised. Does he even exist?"

A laugh rang through the group, but Kier noted an eagerness in the girl's condescension. Maybe at the thought of getting that brood of boarhound.

It would be an incredible feat.

Most of these hunts resulted in one kill, or at most two. After the boys returned, kingsguard would take to the woods with hardier weapons and do the actual job of thinning the heard. But this was ritual. A kicking off. Giving Crat boys small guns and blades and letting them prove something to themselves.

Kier saw Ahren's face redden at the implication that he was lying and felt a surge of protectiveness. Perhaps it was a lingering effect of his time with Delphine.

He thought of her courage, and of next week when he'd leave, and forced his feet to move. As he stepped from the shadows, one of the dogs nosed his pants and gave a sharp yowl.

Heads turned.

"Warrick!" At Ahren's shout, the rest of the group put Kier in sight.

He made himself walk forward. This was why he'd come, after all. *You're Crat tonight. Be a Crat.*

"Nisha, boys, this is Warrick." Ahren's voice was higher. He almost sounded nervous. "Warrick is the one I told you about. He's from...nearby."

Kier was stoic as they looked him over. His fingers roamed to his wrists, feeling the need to check they were covered by his sleeves and gloves.

He could control his shadows well enough when he was with Grimm, but he'd never tested his restraint with others.

"Warrick," Ahren invited.

Seven sets of eyes hung on him. Two lanky boys were mirror images of one another; one of them pulled a red cloth out of his belt and wiped his forehead. A third had his hat tipped sideways, a hand on his small gun. A fourth, built smaller, seemed to prefer his hound's company and hovered at the back of the group.

A fifth boy with hooded eyes assessed Kier, tapping the side of the blade that hung at his waist. "Does he speak?"

"He does." Kier worked his chin up. "Hello. Thank you for inviting me." He cringed at how formal he sounded to his own ears.

Rolling his shoulders, he tried to relax as a few boys nodded in welcome and others traded unreadable looks.

Kier waited for their questions about who he was and where he'd come from.

But the girl—Nisha—held up a hand as she inspected him, a slow grin spreading across her face. She had deep, burnished skin, a square jaw, and hair pulled tight under her hat.

Kier studied the silver crown ring on her thumb as she whispered something in Ahren's ear, encouraging him with a nod.

Ahren came to meet him then. "For you," he said, handing Kier a belt and gun. Just like that.

The weapon felt lighter than it looked.

Around their legs, dogs whined and circled. As horses were led over, Ahren gave him a small smile.

"Welcome to the hunt." He clapped a hand on the back of Kier's neck. Despite the intent stares and Ahren's clammy grip, Kier felt the opposite of what he had in the window of the tutoring room—not a longing, but belonging.

In two lines of four, the hunting party assessed tree-lined paths from where they sat on horses in the middle of the bounty wood. Hounds circled with their noses to the ground, whining to be set free.

One of the twins beside Kier wiped his brow with his red cloth. "Darker than I thought it'd be."

"The dark is part of the challenge," Nisha called from two horses away.

"It's not so bad," Kier said quietly to the worried boy. "Your eyes will adjust. And near the lake, the canopy opens."

The boy nodded appreciatively at him.

Nisha leaned forward on her horse. "You've hunted here?"

Kier felt all their curious eyes on him again.

"No," he admitted quickly. He couldn't tell them the king's commander had taken Kier into the bounty woods many a night to train swords. "I've taken walks here is all, and read about the creatures."

Nisha nudged her steed forward in a circle to face Kier. She was clearly in charge here.

"Have you ever been on a hunt?" she asked him.

Kier thought about lying. But the problem with lies was that they were hard to keep track of. "No, this is my first."

The way Nisha's eyes skittered over Kier made him shift, bracing for questions. *Who are you here with at Gray Castle? Why haven't we seen you in Cirque?* Kier had also prepared for this. With the king's party, there'd be guests from every region at court for the next week. He could feign origins from any. Plenty of high-borns lived in Easton to the south and Kit to the north.

But Nisha only pointed to the woods. "My father has land like this north of Cirque, near Prum. His hunters capture beasts and bring them to our range, so I can practice."

Kier held back his surprise. He'd never met anyone who hunted for sport. Everything brought in from the king's woods fed those at the castle.

"Boarhound are the most dangerous because they don't look ferocious," she told them, though her dark eyes glittered on Kier. "In fact, some could fool you into thinking they're docile... Are you fast on your feet, Warrick?"

Kier bristled at the strange question, and the way she'd said his name. Like it had been a separate question.

Before he opened his mouth to answer, she turned her attention to the rest of the group. "Boarhound attack when threatened. They feign weakness, then ambush. Our best bet is to take one by surprise."

She cracked her neck to one side, then the other, a carnal gleam in her eye. As if she couldn't wait to sink a blade into a boarhound.

Nisha motioned ahead where two paths forked, one leading into the forest, one trailing around it. "We'll split into two groups. Four will take horses on the northern path along the One Sea. It's longer, and the sea is louder; it'll mask the horses. And four will go on foot with the dogs through the woods."

She looked down the line at each of them. "Ahren..."

Beside Kier, the boy with the blazing hair was still, but his brows seemed to ask Nisha a silent question.

She nodded once. "...and Warrick. You two will go with me and Sorin."

At his name, the one with hooded eyes tapping the knife on his belt gave a tight smile. When Nisha slipped down off her horse, he did the same.

"My group will take the woods," she said, her gaze settling between Kier and Ahren. "The rest of you, the north. Look for lairs, and we'll meet at the lake. Remember—boarhound hide where it's darkest. And no shots, unless you're sure you've got your beast."

The night made a dark cloak around them, carving silhouettes of thick-skinned trees with tufted boughs. The particles of magic that liked these woods kept to the canopy, but every so often Kier saw a shimmer.

Sometimes when he walked behind Jory out of these woods back to the castle, Kier would let a shadow lick up. He was intrigued with how the particles moved to it, drawn like little magnets—in curiosity, he hoped, and not in fear of him.

Kier was used to the small noises that crept about in the dark. His eyes and ears were his best advantage. But they seemed to keep Nisha's and Sorin's grips tight on their knives.

Weapons had always felt unnatural in Kier's hands—using his mind was easier. But he couldn't use shadows to slay a boarhound, and he couldn't appear weak, so he tried to hold the gun Ahren gave him as if he knew how to use it. As they roamed, he scoured the foliage between the knotty trees where he imagined boarhound might lie in wait for a taste of the smaller animals that scurried and hopped.

They were walking two by two, with the dogs leading. About halfway to the lake, Kier drew to a stop and motioned to a print in the sod. A thick hoof with four claws. "They cut due east," Kier beamed, expecting Ahren to smirk or clap him on the shoulder again.

Ahren traded looks in the dark with Nisha, who shook her head and continued to the lake.

If the boarhound were hunting, though, Kier doubted they'd find one there. The land around it sloped steeply to water, and trees were sparser. There was less food and fewer places for beasts to hide.

Even the dogs wanted to pull east. But Nisha was the master here, so Kier followed.

A few minutes later, when another set of prints cut their path, the dogs whimpered and raced ahead a bit, zagging left.

When Nisha still didn't stop, a pit grew in Kier's stomach.

"What are we looking for if not tracks?" He turned to Ahren and was surprised to find the boy already watching him. His face looked worried—wrong somehow—in the light of the pink-red moons shining down through the sparser trees.

"I—" Ahren stammered.

"Come on," Sorin barked, and Ahren flinched as if a beast had leaped at him.

"We must be close," Nisha said.

Ahren closed his mouth and slowly loosened his gun from his belt.

Their careful feet, their tense muscles, the looks they kept casting between them—everything was telling Kier something wasn't right. But he was new to this, so maybe he was wrong. He was finding Crats harder to read than Grimm or Delphine, maybe even his uncle. Maybe Ahren, maybe all of them, were as nervous as he was about finding and ending a creature.

A faint squeal sounded in the distance. After a brief pause, Kier heard another. Then the sound of boys shouting.

The dogs tore off with chesty howls.

"Do you think the others found something?" Kier asked. "Should we go help?"

Sorin and Ahren looked at Nisha. He didn't understand why they were hesitating. Was Nisha still set on finding a lair?

"Warrick." She slowed to stop, so they all did. "Where did you say the lake was?"

Three faces turned and shone at him, reddened by the night.

Kier felt his wrists grow cold, and he squeezed the gun in his hand a little tighter, sifting a gaze through the woods. "We should be nearing it." He didn't see any signs of dens here, though. "I don't think we're going to find any—"

"Show us," Nisha demanded, gesturing with a thick arm for him to lead, and Kier saw just how well built she was. Not as muscled as Jory Dagon. But strong. And almost as tall as Kier.

Sorin, tap-tap-tapping the side of his blade, matched her in size.

Kier walked between them all, trying to quell the chill growing under his gloves.

"Don't be stupid."

He wasn't being stupid. He was having faith. Maybe this was what friendship was outside the castle walls. Challenging, jesting, proving oneself...

But when Kier edged ahead of them along the path, he frowned. They were already at the lake. Just a few paces ahead was the crest of the steep slope. The water glittered pink and silver in a wide swath below.

A click made Kier turn his head.

With a tremoring hand, Ahren aimed his gun. Beside him, Sorin and Nisha held their blades.

Kier darted a look around, expecting hooked tusks and a meaty snout.

Sorin chuckled. "I didn't think this would be so easy."

Kier turned his head slowly then and realized they were fixed on *him*. His heart beat faster.

Nisha tilted her head. "You're sure, Ahren? This is the heathen shadow boy you saw?"

Kier met Ahren's eyes, praying this was a joke. A rite of passage in their group.

Ahren swallowed. "It was him. I saw the shadows in the tower, then he came to the window." The gun in his hand shook harder, and his eyes begged something of Kier.

Betrayal burned at Kier's wrists like ice as it hit him how stupid he'd really been. How from the moment Ahren invited him, the only dark creature they'd intended to hunt in the woods...was him.

"I've never seen one up close. How does it work, *heathen*? Do we have to cut it out of you?" Sorin nudged his knife at Kier. "Let's see your shadows."

He remembered the gun in his hand. He didn't want to use it. Would they really hurt him? "I don't know what you're talking about. I'm no one."

Nisha huffed, stepping closer to him. Her eyes darted down the slope.

Kier stepped back and tripped, catching himself before sliding too far. The dark seemed to stir, but not from the night. From inside him.

"You think you're special, don't you?" Nisha asked, her eyes sharp. "My father says you almost destroyed us all. That every Magie should be hunted and put in chains for the centuries you sat the throne and led us into sin."

Sin?

"I don't know anything about those people. I'm just a boy." He looked to Ahren. "Like you. I just wanted to be friends."

Ahren's hand lowered a fraction.

Sorin nudged Nisha, and they both raised their knives.

A flash of concern crossed Ahren's face. "You said you just wanted to meet him. That you wouldn't hurt him."

Nisha ignored him. "Is that it, shadow boy? Are you too afraid to show us who you really are? Because you know what's inside you is unnatural? Let's see it."

Sorin lunged at him, grabbing Kier's wrist.

In a reflex, Kier raised the gun in his hand.

Sorin's eyes only shined in eagerness. "Do it. Pull the trigger."

Kier's heart hammered so fast he couldn't hear his own reply.

Swiftly, Sorin ripped the weapon out of Kier's grasp and spun the barrel around to his own head. With wild eyes, he pulled the trigger against his temple.

One, two, three clicks.

With each, Kier winced.

After the fourth, Sorin threw the gun down the hill and laughed. "Think we'd really give you a weapon?" Leaning closer, he stripped the glove right off Kier's hand.

Kier tightened his fist too late. A coil had already loosened from his pale skin. And before his other hand could clamp his wrist, before he could hide what he was, the three of them clearly saw.

"Look at him!" Sorin jeered. "Freak."

Kier's stomach clenched so hard he couldn't breathe. *Stupid, stupid, stupid.* His gaze dragged through the dark, searching for help.

Something moved in the foliage down wood. He only knew because a wave of particles whirled where it rustled. Almost right away, there came a chorus of barks and howls. Then a sharp squeal that quickly died—as a shot rang out.

Kier's heart leapt while the others' heads whirled. Was the other group close? If he called out, would they help him? Or did they know about Nisha's plan?

Ahren lowered his gun. "Nisha, forget this. Leave him here like you planned, and let's just go."

Nisha spun back, her interest returning to Kier's hand. "I think those at court would be interested to know King Osiris has a Shadowcaster up in his towers."

Kier shook his head. "You can't say anything. Please." It would ruin his uncle, his only family. It could kill Kier. And Delphine... What would happen to her and her brother?

"Hurry this up," Sorin snapped.

"What—what are you going to do?"

Nisha moved her coat aside to extract a small pouch. "I hear when you take a piece off a Magie, it turns to ash. Give me something to show for this hunt, shadow boy, then we'll let you go."

Hate rolled off of her, sending a shiver straight to Kier's neck, where his skin prickled and his hair stood straight.

They lunged at him, grabbing for his arms.

"Ahren!" Kier shouted. "Please!"

Kier tried to shake loose, but they were strong and he was weak. They held him in place.

"Stop moving!" Nisha shouted.

He didn't listen, and in the flurry, Kier felt the unmistakable bite of steel piercing his gut. He pitched forward in sharp pain as someone yanked the blade back out of him.

"You cut him!" Sorin whooped.

Blood, Kier thought, woozy. Surely blood was oozing...

"Get his hand!" Nisha wrestled for it, determined.

"Ahren," Kier gasped for help. "Please."

"I'm sorry," he thought he heard him reply.

I'm sorry, I'm sorry, I'm sorry.

Ahren was sorry. And the truth of what he was sorry for turned Kier's stomach as he continued to struggle against them. Ahren had lured him there. He never intended to be his friend.

He was loyal to the two who were hurting him. Who wanted a piece of him. Who maybe wanted to kill him.

What would the king say?

Kier wasn't supposed to be out here.

As the woods seemed to sway, he could feel his uncle's hand across his cheekbone all over again. He could see Bridgen's hard eyes on him. *You're bleeding on the floor.* He could see Ahren's smirk in the hall—he'd already known what Kier was. Lies, lies, lies.

Kier felt the sear of a blade again, this time across the top of his hand. Still he fought against them. He would not be a trophy. He would not be prey.

"Nisha, stop!" Ahren lurched forward, pulling at her arm. "You swore you wouldn't. I never would've—"

Nisha shook him off.

"Hold still, freak." Sorin.

Freak.

He'd wanted acceptance. He'd wanted a night out of the dark.

Heathen.

He didn't belong. He should've listened.

Unnatural.

Now, he was going to die here.

Unless.

The darkness roused in him, promising a storm.

As they pulled at him, as the knives kept nicking at his thumb, as his nausea kept swelling, Kier was suddenly burning, but not with fire—with the coldest chill of ice—as if he'd been swept into an arctic sea. As he landed there in that freezing place, his shadows burst from his bones. In a heavy, seeking mist, they spread out and across the woods.

He saw a flash of terrified eyes—first Nisha's, and Sorin's, then Ahren's, too. Ahren, who did look sorry.

In the moment before Kier stumbled at their sudden release of him and pitched down the sloping hill, the three of them were eaten up by darkness.

And the woods went silent.

Chapter 4
We Who Are Hunted
Gray Castle, Cirque
Thirty-Five Years Ago

He'd killed them.

He'd *obliterated* them.

As he fell, and was bumped and rolled down the hill to the lakes' edge, Kier felt the stab of the shocking truth, along with every sharp rock and branch that littered the ground.

He faded. In, out, for a minute or maybe more, until his skin felt numb where the water met it, and he lost track of where he hurt and bled.

In his mind's eye, Kier saw each of their faces right before they'd pushed him to breaking and darkness had unleashed itself from him.

A distant squeal.

Kier's eyes flashed open. From his vantage, the silvery lake and a few red trees were tilted sideways. There were sounds—a huffing and rattling of something struggling to breathe.

It didn't sound human.

They'd walked an hour to get here. He was an hour from help.

Forcing his hands to bear his weight, Kier stifled a cry and shoved out of the muck. When his gut screamed and his head grew light, Kier pressed a shaky hand to his stomach, where he felt a gaping wound. Struggling from his knees onto his feet, he eyed the sharp hill he'd fallen down.

Tree roots jutted from the earth, offering a way up if he could stay conscious.

Staggering forward through the pain, he pulled at roots with his free hand, clawing up the slope.

At the top, the cloying scent of death met Kier.

His eyes fell to the boot prints—signs of his own struggle that marked heels through dirt.

Nearby, a round object caught his eye. It was a hunter's hat, or half of one. At some point, he'd lost the one he'd been wearing. But this one... It was Nisha's.

And, nearby...a hand.

At the sight of the unmistakable shape, Kier's breath vanished. A rancid taste filled his mouth.

It was a hand that, hours ago, Kier had shaken in a gesture of supposed friendship, when Ahren invited him into their group.

Gripping his wound, Kier heaved. When his stomach was empty, he wiped a string of spit on the sleeve of his borrowed coat and made himself face what he'd done.

Pink and meaty...and blackened where it had been severed from Ahren's wrist.

He did that. His shadows. Now three young Crats wouldn't return from the hunt, and who would everyone blame?

"My representatives are mortals. They have notions about your kind."

Kier frantically looked around, weighing where to go and what to do, when something cried in the night.

Rooted in place, he tracked the sounds to rustling foliage as a soft stomp of hoofbeats rode in his direction.

A creature the size of a large dog limped into view from the east. The moment it met the moons' light, Kier recognized its pit-dark eyes and curving tusks.

The boarhound's thick, humped pelt was matted on one of its shoulders. As it set its sights on Kier, he braced for its charge, knowing he had nothing left in him for a physical fight.

But after another step, the beast's front legs gave out. Its body buckled to the ground and Kier saw it was blood that matted its fur. An agonizing cry ripped from its throat and sounded across the night, spearing itself through Kier's own chest.

Its horrid squeals gave way to whimpers as the boarhound's chest shuddered.

Kier looked at the predator-turned-prey, lying on its side. It was a creature of night, like him. It'd been hunted, like him. Now, it was about to die alone, like...

The boarhound watched him, taking a long, ragged breath. Then it stilled.

After a few moments, smaller squeals chirped like weeping bells in the distance.

"A mother and her brood."

Kier's wrists went cold. He felt death everywhere. He almost didn't hear the voices.

"It went this way!"

"Are you sure?"

Hope and fear thrust at him like double swords. The shadows that'd killed Ahren, Nisha, and Sorin hadn't reached the northern trail!

Kier wasn't alone out here. The others were alive.

He tried to remember how the rest of the group had looked at him, at the tent and on the horses. Maybe they hadn't known about Nisha's plan to hurt him. Maybe they'd help him now.

Maybe—

Stupid.

These were the kind of thoughts that made him ignore his instincts. Surely the others must've known. If they saw him, they'd only run ahead to tell the kingsguards, their Crat families, and the representatives, proving Nisha was right—that Magies were dangerous.

A soft ringing sounded between Kier's ears. It warbled like a bird's call, light and worried.

Relief rolled through him.

He knew the sound of Delphine's summons well after two years. But his gaze slid to Ahren's detached hand. If it was discovered, if magic was suspected, what would happen to those at the castle who were Magie?

They would suffer for the crime.

He let Delphine's summons go unanswered. Feeling sick, he bit his lip and held his gut harder, then nudged the severed hand with his boot to move it toward the hill's edge.

"Nisha!"

Kier froze at the voice, coming from the east.

"Sorin!" another called.

He moved faster, toeing at the limb. But its fingers dragged in the dirt, as if they didn't want to go.

He had to pick it up, to throw it, but bending to do so felt impossible.

"You could probably heal yourself, you know..."

Kier stilled at the echo of Delphine's wisdom. Yes. He would try.

Drawing his hand away from his gut, he tore open his shirt, ignoring the distant calls of the others, the sound of creatures skittering, and the birds flapping overhead.

He felt for the chill in his bones.

For long seconds, as the call to his affinity went unanswered, Kier panicked that there was nothing left to pull—that what he'd done earlier had left him empty.

But with his next breath, they were there.

Not curious coils, like those that'd raced up the tutoring room stairs. And not the frightening...mist. These were silken tendrils, gentle as a hug.

Kier turned them on himself, pressing the darkness to his flesh. He was no healer. But his shadows settled there, in his wound, like a bandage. A temporary reprieve. His stomach numbed instantly, and the pain receded.

"Ahren! Nisha!" the voices called closer.

Kier lunged for the hand. Biting back guilt, he heaved Ahren's remains as hard as he could down the hill, picturing those sorry eyes.

When it plunged into the lake, Kier reeled in the opposite direction, letting his boots smear the mess of footprints in the dirt as he bowed his head, passing the dead boarhound, and set a course in the direction they'd come earlier. When Kier thought this was just a night out of the dark.

How quickly he was learning. There was no leaving the darkness when the darkness was in you.

The voices faded.

He lumbered, sticking close to the trees. Just when he thought his legs might give out, Kier saw a glow. A few paces more, and there were the torches bathing Gray Castle's courtyard.

Voices still spilled from the hunting tent. And music, too, farther away—the king's party.

There were too many obstacles standing between Kier and the path to his chambers, including the two men still occupying chairs outside the tent, clasping mugs and awaiting the hunters' return.

Hunts could last till morning. These men would be happy to drink and wait until then. They would see him if he fled now.

If he could muster more shadows, he could risk subduing the pair, or...he could use what he'd already cast.

Kier sank carefully to his knees and glanced at the canopy above where particles shimmered. Grimm had taught him how to hide, and to choose the smartest path.

He huffed a few shallow breaths, then called the tendrils from his wound.

He groaned as they peeled away and gathered near his hands. Kier threw his focus to the darkness and, somehow, it grew, until it nearly enveloped him whole.

With a flick of a heavy hand, he sent it to scare the particles up through the trees.

Magic burst from the canopy with a flourish. As Kier grunted forward onto his hands, he saw one of the men outside the tent nudge the other, pointing to the trees.

Yes. Go investigate.

The moment they tottered off toward a pair of horses, Kier seized his chance. This would hurt, he realized, before leaping from his cover.

Feeling along the south wall, he heard the faint shrills of birds circling, but no people, and he staggered to the slim gap in the stonework behind a tree.

It wasn't until he reached the path to the kitchens, where servants flitted about inside, that Kier's vision winked and his head floated, light as air. He collapsed.

The warbling in his mind returned—Delphine.

Kier's eyes went white as bone, as he reached across space to answer her.

"Kier, where are you? I came to your room—" In his mind, he saw her stop, and Kier knew she was seeing him lying there, bleeding. That she'd put together where he'd been.

Through the line between their minds, this gift bestowed to those with affinities in the Witchist order, Kier saw her rush from his washroom.

She was far more practiced than he was at splitting attention between a summons and her surroundings.

There in moments, she dragged Kier as best as she could by the boots, into the natural shadows.

As he fought the blood loss, a murder of black creatures flapped their wings in the glow of the torchlights. Daws. Sentient and swift, they were the king's eyes and ears around the castle.

Delphine quickly settled beside him, and Kier breathed the truth to her. "They're dead. I—I had to—"

"Shhh," she warned, tugging his borrowed coat open wider to lay a hand over his wound. "You never know who's listening."

Chapter 5
Monsters In Our Skin

Gray Castle, Cirque
Thirty-Five Years Ago

Warmth roused him.

Kier's eyes opened on candlelight combing its fingers along his chamber ceiling. At the tingling across his stomach, he rolled his head sideways.

Delphine, biting her lip in concentration, hovered over him, her hands on his gut. "You're awake," she muttered, eyes flitting to his face before refocusing on the task at hand, her shoulders leaking some of their tension. "The wound's taking longer to seal because I didn't heal it all at once," she said.

Of course. They'd almost been interrupted by servants. The first mending had been enough to get Kier to his feet, at least, and with an arm slung over Delphine's shoulders, he'd staggered up the back staircase and through a hidden passageway to his room.

He must've passed out when they got there.

As she leaned over him, long strands loose of Delphine's braid grazed Kier's bare chest. "It's going to scar," she noted.

Kier didn't bother to tell her it already had, deep inside.

He tensed against pricking sensations. By their intensity, he could tell the wound to his gut was far worse than his cut hand earlier.

Nisha's knife must've severed muscle.

Still, it wasn't half as bad as the guilt that needled him. "I'm a murderer," he rasped aloud.

Saying it seemed to split him in two. There was a Kier he might have been—a man with a moral heart—and the Kier he was now—a dangerous creature with no control.

Delphine's hands pulled away, taking her warmth with them.

For an instant, Kier feared she'd leave, and he snatched her wrist. His wild eyes clung to hers. *Don't go*, they begged.

But Delphine winced at where he gripped her, tighter than he'd meant to.

He retracted his hand and forced his eyes upward, taking long breaths to calm his panic.

"Kier," Delphine started.

He nodded to the painting that stretched the ceiling. "Some nights I wonder why he left that after he took the throne."

Grimm's lessons, dictated by the king, rarely touched on the histories that'd always fascinated Kier. He was to focus on the future—learning military strategy, mapmaking, weaponry, and how to control his affinity.

When Delphine didn't answer, he looked at her. She was peering toward the door, as if listening to be sure the halls were quiet.

Satisfied, she climbed onto the bed and lay beside him.

The left side of his body flamed with the heat of her, but he returned his gaze to the depiction of the gods.

Selene was brushed with rich bronze skin, jade eyes, and a storm of curls threaded with vines and flowers. Luna was portrayed more stoically, all muscle with shining metal armor, so marmoreal. And Erebus... The god of the spellers' order that

Kier belonged to was painted with a plume of shadows at his back that looked nearly like wings. It was his mischievous smile and bone-white skin, carved like marble, that intrigued Kier most.

He wondered what a god of darkness might be thinking.

All three sat watching from their thrones, each holding one object: a dagger, an amulet, or a stone. Kier had always wondered about them, too.

Beside him, Delphine sighed. "Maybe His Majesty likes the reminder of what he freed Magus from."

"'Gods who abandoned their creation.'" His voice was thick with sarcasm.

"Gods who let Magus 'descend into chaos,'" she replied in a mimicry of the king's words.

His almost-smirk fell. That was what Kier had done tonight. Descended into chaos.

As he studied Erebus, he thought of the way his shadows had lashed at the quill in his hand earlier, after the tip pierced his flesh in the tutoring room.

If he thought about it, they'd been coming to his defense recently. More, the nearer he got to *Asenti*.

But the way they'd risen to defend him against Nisha and Sorin? That was something else. Something more.

Neither the king nor Grimm had ever mentioned mist...or whatever it had been.

Music drifted through the window then, as if someone at the king's party had opened a balcony door.

"It's getting late, Delphine. You should get to your chambers. To Rhodin," Kier said, though his throat squeezed at the thought of her going, of being alone with what he'd done.

When he looked at her, her eyes were soft on him. "I had one of the kitchen girls tuck Rhodin in, after I discovered you were gone. I had a feeling..." She shook her head. "Anyway, he's safe."

He swallowed, relieved. "I was so naïve tonight... So—"

"Good," she supplied, shifting to her side and lifting a hand to brush his midnight hair from his forehead.

Kier closed his eyes a moment, reveling in her touch. A dark thought made him pull back. "You're lying beside a killer."

At that, she pushed up on an elbow, pressing a hand firmly against his chest. "They provoked you, Kier. They branded you a monster to convince themselves the monster wasn't them."

Monster. The word was powerful off her tongue. Certainly not meek. Not like when they'd called him a freak.

But Kier's worry from the woods crept over him. Could he trust himself to be near another person? Aside from which, it was only a matter of time before the three were discovered missing and an investigation would commence.

He knew what he should do. What a good man would do.

"They're going to find out," he said. "Either they'll find something I missed or someone from the hunt might see me at *Asenti* this week and ask questions. If they suspect it might have been a Magie, they'll come after all magic-born, even you, but if I confess it was me—"

"Then the king would be forced to kill you, and you'd ruin his plan for his new army," she interrupted, narrowing her eyes at him. "Then we'd be worse off, wouldn't we?"

He swallowed. He hadn't thought of that.

"If you're a monster because you're Magie, then so are we all. So am I," she said.

"Never." Kier shook his head, taking her cheek in his hand. "You couldn't hurt anyone. Not like I can."

Delphine sat up all the way, her eyes shining on him like glass. "Anyone is capable of anything under the right circumstances, and if you tell yourself you're a monster, you'll start believing it. So don't. You aren't. Good is what evil preys on best. Those Crats would've murdered you if you'd let them. So confess what you must—to me—then let this go. Never speak of it again."

She looked wildly at him, so impassioned that Kier wondered if Delphine could hear his thudding heart.

She was beautiful with that heated gaze pinning him to the bed, and it stirred a great deal more than his shadows. Need. It stirred need. "I have nothing more to confess."

Their eyes locked one long moment before Kier couldn't wait any longer. Sweeping a hand behind her neck to pull her down to him, he claimed her lips.

It was a reckless, untamed kiss at first. And when her tongue slipped inside Kier's mouth, he let everything go, everything but her.

It was a fury wholly different than the hurried, forbidden kisses in a wash room. It was two young lovers on the cusp of being grown, realizing how fast everything could end, refusing to go to their graves with a single regret.

Delphine broke away to catch a breath. Then her lips found his jaw, kissing a breathy trail up the sloping edge of it before reclaiming his mouth. She nipped at his lip, slowly, as if they had all the time in the world.

She was fire. She was beautiful torture.

He let the sensation of her warm lips and her acceptance of his dark nature settle in his bones alongside his shadows. Between heated-filled kisses, he let her seal away his guilt and heal his conscience, same as she'd healed his physical wounds.

He wasn't a freak or unnatural. Not with her. As long as he had her, he'd never be unloved. He'd never be the villain.

He threaded his fingers through the loose strands of her braid, tugging it, seizing the moment to deepen their kiss.

They'd learned how to love, how to express feelings, together. Only with each other. She was his. *His.*

She hastily crawled atop his lap, letting her dress hitch around her hips, and Kier's hands traveled to her backside, tracing the swell of her curves through the fabric.

When she rocked forward and a soft moan spilled into his mouth, he fisted the material in his hands, wishing there was nothing—not a shred of clothing—between them.

It was a storm waking up in him, the way he needed her.

Breathing hard, he broke the kiss, just long enough to ask with his eyes if this was heading where he thought. If she could truly want it, too.

She nodded fervently, already reaching beneath her skirts to untie the fabric between her legs.

Kier wrestled with his own pants, fumbling with the column of buttons down the high waist. "Delphine," he breathed as he tugged. There were probably precautions to consider. What did people do?

But she pressed a finger to his lips, then kissed him there, and he was lost in her heat again.

He'd figured they'd be older or married when they shared this bond, but the world was cruel, and some didn't survive past eighteen. Nothing was promised—not for their kind—so he kissed her, surrendering to their caressing tongues, their teeth clipping together in a frenzy.

Delphine leaned back to work her dress up higher, out of the way.

He shuddered at the sight of her golden, bare skin, then again at the first feel of her softness against his thighs as she shifted to position herself just shy of where his length was hardening.

Kier looked up at her. He had to see her, watch her accept him this way, for the first time. He had to see her love him.

Delphine's chest rose in quick breaths. Her lips tugged into a grin as she saw him drinking her in. She edged her hips forward, until he felt her warmth, right there.

He nearly combusted when her hand grasped him, when her head fell back and she sank down onto him. His breath shuddered at the feel of her—hot, tight, enveloping him.

Grasping her thighs, Kier watched her intently, every twitch of her mouth, every blink of her eyes as he thrust his hips and buried himself in her. He felt the moment the tightness gave way with her small wince.

Then she was moving on him.

"Kier." The look on her face was pure awe as she braced a hand on his chest, and he was sure without looking that his expression was a mirror of her pleasure.

Her hands roved impatiently to his shoulders, wrapping his neck to pull him up to sit with her.

As their mouths met again, Kier rocked his hips, holding her closer, hoping he was doing this right.

Her answering moan, her nails biting the skin at his back, spurred him on. Again. Again.

Too soon, he felt a climbing inside him, a crescendo as quick as his lashing shadows, as quick as the pace Delphine was setting on his lap.

Just as they crested a peak, as he fisted a hand around her braid and his teeth grazed her neck, as she called out his name and shuddered against him, as he met his own feverish release, Kier's chamber doors burst open and the candlelight snuffed with a draft of air.

Delphine gasped.

In a reflex, Kier whirled her off him and back against the pillows, shielding her as a brigade of boots stomped into his room.

He hurried to do up his pants.

"It's far too late to hide your sins." The king's voice belted across the room.

When Kier turned, he saw a glinting crown and menacing blue eyes fixed their way. His uncle wore his best robes, bejeweled and fit for a party.

He stopped a half-dozen paces from Kier's bed, and Kier's eyes widened when he saw the shrewd bird on his shoulder. Its glassy eyes glared at Kier before it leapt to soar out the open window.

Jory Dagon, flanked by three guards in silver armor, stepped from the throng of soldiers blocking Kier's door to the king's side.

Kier's pulse pounded. He recognized the trio of kingsguards. They were present at sentencings.

Kier quickly bowed his head. "This is my fault. Don't punish her." The king had told him not to let anyone too close. How obvious, from their state, the mussed bed, and the scents in the room, that Kier had broken that rule.

But when he glanced up, he saw the king wasn't focused on their bare skin.

His uncle waved an angry arm toward the window and lunged a step forward. "What did you do in the woods?" His seething words were a vicious whisper.

Kier's eyes snapped to the window, then back to his uncle. "The daw…"

"Yes, the daw! It was but one that watched you return from the woods. And do you know what else it saw? The hunters, just returned, reporting their missing companions to my soldiers."

The king lumbered another few steps.

Jory shadowed him.

"Are"—the king let the word slap—"they"—another sharp pause—"dead?"

Kier made himself still. He hadn't much practice lying to his uncle, today notwithstanding, and his hesitation gave him away.

"What you've done warrants a public death by my order—for you and anyone who aided you!" The king's violent eyes groped to Delphine.

Kier panicked. "No. She only healed me. She had no idea of anything else. Uncle…"

The king turned his head, giving silent command to Jory, whose thick brows folded together. His crystalline eyes kept watch on Kier as if he weren't the young, disobedient nephew of the king, but a cornered boarhound. Then he motioned to the trio of guards, who were already unsheathing their narrow lengths of steel.

Delphine's sharp breaths behind Kier snapped his composure.

Scrabbling off the bed in only pants and bare feet, he made a shield in front of her and felt his shadows stir as the guards approached, blades at the ready.

And then he did feel like a cornered creature of the night.

The monster in Kier bled out through his skin. Black coils traveled the length of both his arms, clinging, waiting.

The guards slowed, trading nervous looks. They'd known what Kier was, but they'd never seen him unleash his darkness.

Kier himself had just seen how deadly it could be, and it had terrified him, too.

"Let her go to her chambers," he implored the king quietly. "Speak with me alone."

Jory shifted at his king's side. "Their families will demand punishment, Your Grace."

The king's eyes clouded as they studied Kier and his outstretched arms that leached shadow.

"Look at you," his uncle said. "How do I make you captain of my army if you can't control yourself? How do I ever claim you as my own if you cannot obey?"

The disapproval of Kier's only family was another knife in his gut.

Shoulders sagging, Kier dropped his arms.

"Stay," he commanded the darkness inside him, while it still felt within his control, and it seeped back into his skin.

"Uncle—" he began. "Majesty. It will never happen again. I swear it."

"No," the king snapped. "It will not." He nodded to his kingsguards. "Bring me the girl."

With the shadows gone, the trio rushed at Kier. In an instant, three blades were at his neck.

A handful more guards drew forward, with guns, and roughly snatched Delphine from the bed.

Kier opened his mouth, but she flashed him a look, giving her head a quick shake.

But he couldn't help it. "Take me," he cried. "Take me. Take anyone else! Not her. Not her!"

Kier had no one but her, save for Grimm and his uncle. When he left for the army, he knew Delphine would wait for him. She was his. That the king might harm her stirred the monster in his skin again.

"If you kill her, I'll never forgive you," he dared threaten. "I'll die before I lead your army."

The king threw up a hand to halt the guards with Delphine. It was a long moment before he tilted his head. "You wish her to live? Then so be it."

Kier's shoulders released their tension as the king's gaze slid to Jory and he commanded, "Bring him in."

Him?

Jory's face crumpled. "Majesty, are you sure?"

"Don't question me."

Kier's mind raced. "Uncle?"

"Someone must pay," the king mumbled as Jory left. Looking at Kier, he added, "And someone must learn. Remember the next time you think to disobey me that this was your doing."

A sickening feeling coiled itself around Kier's stomach, and as a set of small feet padded into the room it tore up his throat, a creature desperate for air. Kier's mouth burned with bile as a confused Rhodin—golden hair mussed and rubbing sleepy eyes—was brought to the king.

His uncle put a hand on the boy's shoulder. Then the king of Magus extracted a small blade from his royal robes.

A blade Kier had seen once before.

"Rhodin!" Delphine's shrill scream rang in his ears, and the soldiers forced her to her knees.

Kier lunged, but his throat was met with pricking steel.

A flick of a wrist, and he'd be dead.

He was shaking, chilled to the bone with shadows pressing against his skin, demanding release, as Delphine called out, "No! Kier! Do something!"

"*Don't*," Jory warned in his ear. Kier hadn't seen the commander approach, but he was there, a brute wall coming around to block Kier's view.

There was a trace of sympathy in his eyes as he said quietly, "If you want the girl to live, you will sacrifice tonight."

"No—"

"This is the way he shows his love, Kier. With a lesson, instead of your death. This way," Jory said, glancing over his shoulder and back, "he doesn't have to lose you. So take it. Take his mercy."

Mercy? "What is he going to do to him?"

Jory's brow arched, and Kier pictured what he knew the blade could do—what he'd witnessed the first day he'd seen his uncle siphon magic out of someone.

Jory had tried to stop him then, tried to find another way for the king to achieve two desired ends—making Magies obedient and sustaining the king's own strength.

But Jory did not try to stop him now.

"Convince him. I know you can. Convince my uncle to take me instead."

Jory looked fairly sorry then. But if there was anyone loyal to the king, it was the leader of his Royal Army. The man who sometimes shared his uncle's bed. "It is him today, or Delphine."

There came a slash of skin and a small cry. The sound of long, thick draws of air. The thud of Kier's own heart in his ears. The whimpers...sniffling, gasping sounds from a boy who couldn't hear his sister's sobs filling the chambers.

But Kier could hear it...and do nothing but sink to the floor.

"Don't let love make you weak," his uncle had told him three years ago, on a night Kier found a small hound hit by an army wagon and a guard had to put a bullet between its eyes. "Sometimes death is the best mercy."

If love made you weak, Kier was.

He couldn't stop this now. Because, he realized, if he saved her brother, he condemned Delphine. And while he didn't fear dying, he was afraid of living without her, with no one to love him.

Weak.

His shadows heaved against his skin, as if telling Kier there was one way to end this.

But, no.

No.

As he shook with the effort of containing his affinity, Kier pictured the mist in the woods and what it'd done when he snapped. A few hours ago, he could hardly stomach the idea of killing a boarhound. Then his shadows had killed three people.

He couldn't let his darkness out, not with Delphine here.

He couldn't trust what he'd do.

At a rush of air through the open window, white ash swirled across the floor to meet his pale hands and he knew it was done.

Jory stepped aside, and Kier watched Delphine dragged from his chambers.

He'd told his shadows to stay.

Now Rhodin was gone.

Jory called the trio of soldiers off Kier, and they filed out of the room past the king.

His uncle was stooped, breathing hard, and Kier forced himself to watch as Rhodin's life—his stolen magic—restored the king's youth.

When the monarch straightened, looking far younger than his forty years, something unfurled in Kier. Something angry and sharp and eager to break men apart. Something welcomed by his shadows.

Hatred, Kier thought, as the king rolled his neck and sauntered toward him.

Even as he glared at his uncle, his weakness—his love for a girl—spilled out. "Where are they taking her?"

The king turned a brief moment, motioning Jory to leave them. Then returning his attention, he said, "The girl will be moved to another post."

He felt a surge of panic.

"She won't be harmed if you listen," his uncle said. "You'll breathe no word of tonight to anyone. And I'm expediting your

Asenti. In three days, you'll be a soldier of the crown and think no more of love." He spit that last word, as if it'd wronged him.

Kier felt like cowering. But for Delphine, for Rhodin, for the day in the future when Kier would not be weak, he held his gaze. "Why wouldn't you kill me?"

For the briefest moment, the king's gaze grew distant, as if his thoughts were elsewhere. "Just like your mother," he muttered.

"My mother?" The king hadn't spoken of Kier's parents in years. All he knew was they'd died in the war, when he was just two years old.

But the king hadn't heard him, or didn't care. "Your life is too valuable to waste," he said.

Kier flinched at the word—*valuable*. And the implication Rhodin's life hadn't been.

The king crouched, shocking Kier by placing a hand on his shoulder. "You want me to claim you?"

Did he, anymore?

He wished he didn't.

"Prove your place in this kingdom. Serve this crown, earn the trust of the monarchy, and I will acknowledge you as I've promised. Perhaps I'll even let you claim what your heart desires."

Kier's heart thumped with hope, but just as swiftly an instinct waking up inside him warned not to trust his uncle's words.

He said nothing as the king left. Nothing when the door shut and he heard guards settle against the walls outside his chambers.

Kier pushed up off his knees and back to rest against his bed, putting his head in his hands.

Where had they taken her? She must be dying with the pain of losing her brother. She'd raised Rhodin, despite her father being here at the castle.

Kier dropped his hands.

Would the king have taken her to him in the west tower? It was too terrible to think about.

It was all too terrible.

He shoved to his feet in search of a shirt, pulling it over his sweat-soaked skin as he rushed across the room to find boots. Then he gathered supplies and, where ash still coated his floor, he swept the remains into a vase.

He knew what the king said. Obey. Prove yourself. Leave the girl alone.

But there was another choice.

With the vase and a bag on his back, Kier faced the northern wall in his chambers where a bookshelf stretched. Splitting the span of the shelves was a painting as tall as him, two unlit candelabras perched on either side of it. Art that the king had gifted Kier on his tenth birthday.

A portrait of his uncle on the throne.

Kier tipped the frame sideways, then, like darkness itself, slipped into the passageway.

Chapter 6
Down Forbidden Halls

GRAY CASTLE, CIRQUE
THIRTY-FIVE YEARS AGO

Kier stared down the forbidden west wing.

The walls seemed to lean in, waiting to see if he had the courage to defy the king.

He stepped forward.

A trilling between his ears made him veer off balance, and Kier nearly plunged down the winding staircase where just hours ago he'd met Ahren.

It trilled louder, and he nearly dropped the vase in his arms.

Grimm Hermes's summons was a siren compared to Delphine's. Kier was forced to sit on a step and let Grimm into his mind's eye.

With no preamble, the Spellcaster snapped, "Stay where you are," as his grave expression filled Kier's vision.

He could tell Grimm was in the castle, somewhere close.

"No." Kier gritted his teeth, getting to his feet again, trying to sever the connection.

But Grimm wasn't a Spellcaster easily shaken, and Kier wasn't an ascended Magie yet. He lurched forward, bracing a shoulder against the wall to keep himself upright as he walked into the hall, the thought of Delphine driving him onward.

"You're planning to leave with the girl," Grimm said, and Kier stilled, hearing footsteps and the stamp of a cane coming up the stairs behind him.

A moment later, his mind cleared, and there stood Grimm in his fine robes, dressed as his uncle had been, for a party.

"I was with the king when he received the daw," Grimm explained quietly. "Come."

Grimm glanced behind them, but it was late; the nearest sounds in the castle echoed far off, from the laundry and kitchens.

Grimm pulled Kier into a narrow alcove just around the staircase. There, his lips murmured and he raised his spellstaff.

When he did, Kier felt a shudder of energy through him. It lingered, tingling in his fingertips and feet. "What was that?"

"Assurance we won't be seen or heard."

Kier's heart hammered as he followed Grimm into the hall. Beyond the staircase from where they'd come, two kingsguards were marching their way. Kier froze and readied himself to run or draw his shadows, but Grimm merely stood there calmly until the guards passed them.

For a moment, Kier forgot his mission and looked at Grimm in awe. "You just—"

"Cloaked us, yes," Grimm said. "I overheard what happened in the woods. What did the king do to you that you'd risk everything now?"

Kier swallowed around the lump in his throat. "He killed a boy to punish me. Delphine's brother. I begged him to punish me instead, and he refused. Now he's put her somewhere, and

I..." Gripping the vase in one arm, he raised his free hand, then let it fall again. "I can't go lead my uncle's army and pretend he'll ever care for me. I can't leave her here. I'm getting Delphine out, and—"

"You've every right to be livid, but fleeing would be an irrevocable mistake."

Kier's hackles raised. "Don't say my uncle was teaching me a lesson—that he loves me in his way. Jory beat you to it."

Grimm shook his head. "On the contrary. He was too much in love once and it made him afraid."

"My uncle loves no one. He only cares about keeping his crown."

"Fear can make men do terrible things to regain a semblance of the control they lose in loving." Grimm rested a hand on Kier's shoulder. "Your uncle fears losing his crown, and for good reason. Now, come."

Kier glanced down the hall, feeling a tug, an ache to run toward the tower where Delphine's father worked, where he thought she might be. But Grimm was motioning toward the prison doors straight ahead. Who would his tutor want him to see in the prison? Did he know Delphine was there?

"Tell me how you did it, Kier," Grimm glanced at him as they walked. "The young hunters. Tell me how you did it."

Kier stiffened in his stride, gripping the vase tighter. "Because you think me a danger?"

"Because it's you who's in danger."

Nearing the middle of the hall, Kier pictured the look in Nisha's eyes. Sorin's. Ahren's. Before the shadow mist burst from Kier.

The truth spilled out.

When he was finished, Grimm slowed his gait, turning crystal eyes on Kier's. "How long have your shadows been protecting you?"

For some reason, Kier had a hard time holding Grimm's gaze. "A few months."

Grimm nodded. "I've come from conversations at your uncle's party. There are things about the Special Army and its purpose you must know."

"Its purpose is to make Magies safer."

Grimm didn't smile. He began walking again, robes a flurry. "Its sole purpose will be to bring magic to heel. Hundreds of soldiers with the responsibility of ensuring children grow up serving the crown without question. There are hundreds of thousands of Magies across this kingdom. The army will scour every inch of it for children with an affinity and bring them to the king's academy, as capacity allows. At sixteen, younger than you are now, they'll be sent to serve in the military, education, trade, or agriculture. If they don't die before *Asenti*."

Kier could nearly feel the color drain from his face. "*Die*."

He pictured the ash on his feet.

Grimm's cane stamped harder on the marble as they hurried. "As I've told you, it's getting more dangerous for our people. If you flee tonight, you'll have a target on you, all your life, and you'll leave the leadership of the new army in the hands of Magies willing to be far more brutal. More children will die. Your uncle's power will grow. As will the pressure on him to continue his persecution of our kind. He's chosen his side, Kier, and they'll make him prove his loyalty."

Grimm paused again in the hall. "If you stay, if you're patient, if you refuse to let your uncle and this world blacken your heart, you may just change things—from inside."

The bag loosened off Kier's shoulders as he sagged. "But I love her." It was a selfish plea. Grimm was telling him many would die, and he was clinging to his own crusade.

Grimm's gaze was unwavering. "Which is why you need to hear what else I discovered."

Something flickered around Grimm, at the same time tingles rippled through Kier, like the cloak might be waning.

Grimm beckoned him faster. "What you did in the woods with the shadows is called misting. Something I've seen only one other Shadowcaster do in my lifetime."

His heart cantered. "What?"

"You're not an ordinary Shadowcaster, Kier. You're far more."

His mind scrambled to grasp the implication, as Grimm stopped at the end of the hall, short of the iron door gating the prison tunnels.

But Grimm's interest was fixed on a narrow staircase that'd come into view, one that wound behind a hidden alcove.

"I'd be killed on sight for bringing you here, or breathing a word of this. Then the new academy, like the army, would fall to sages all too willing to do what the crown asks in order to safeguard their own positions. But, at the top of those stairs, you'll find the answer to why your uncle's afraid for his throne. What he loves, and why he fears you."

"Fears me? If that were true, he'd have taken me instead of Rhodin."

Grimm merely raised his spellstaff. "If you've the strength to stay, follow those stairs to the last door."

"You've seen what's up there?"

Grimm bowed his head. "I was asked to strengthen wards there, after your uncle saw you in this hall. He's brought me into his circle, Kier, and I've learned to play my role. As will you."

Kier looked to the vase in his arms. "Rhodin... His remains."

The flicker came again around Grimm, and the tingles in Kier.

Grimm took the vase, settling it in his arms. "I'll see she gets them."

"I need to see her, Grimm."

"You must first make the choice whether to stay. With your mind, not your heart," he said sternly and motioned again to the stairs.

Taking a long breath, Kier turned.

He felt the moment the Spellcaster disappeared, when Kier's cloak fizzled out. He sometimes forgot the sage was so powerful that he could create passages and disappear at will.

Kier frowned. Grimm could've offered to passage him and Delphine out of the castle. But he hadn't. The sage had never steered Kier wrong before, though. He ought to at least see what secrets awaited him.

With trepidation and eagerness rousing his shadows, he climbed.

Chapter 7
Throne Of Lies
Gray Castle, Cirque
Thirty-five Years Ago

The door Kier stood before was different.

Forged of iron, impenetrable bounty wood, and odd metal that shimmered amber to blue to green, it arched two feet above his head. There was no knocker and no knob, but something glistened around its seams. A ward.

Kier bent to peer inside a single, gaping lock. He imagined his uncle kept the only key.

There was no way in. So what did Grimm expect him to see?

A chill skated along his wrist. Before he could stop it, a shadow snaked loose and lashed through the keyhole. Kier felt a sharp tug in his mind—like a summons, except he couldn't just see inside the vast chambers. Instead, he sensed everything as the shadow swept the space.

This was new.

He focused, taking it in.

He'd expected a cell, given the room's proximity to the prisons, but it was nearly the size of his own room. Unlike his ever-tidied chambers, though, it had a methodical sort of chaos. Tables were positioned at odd angles, strewn with books laid carefully open. Bowls and herbs were set out in abundance, abandoned but waiting. Candles cluttered every surface, burning and dripping to form waxy piles.

It would drive his uncle mad to spend any time here.

Who could be inside?

His shadow stretched in sunlight sifting through barred windows that were bookended by curtains matching the room's deep-green walls. The light fell over chairs, sofas, bookstacks, and coarse fur rugs, and though he wasn't in the room, he could *feel* its warmth.

The room held two hearths, too, both crackling with fires. At one of them, a chair was rocking.

Then something squawked. A gray bird, pecking suet on a golden perch in the corner.

In the chair, someone admonished, "Shhh."

Kier went still, though his shadow pressed on, toward the person whose curtain of dark hair—with a single gray swath—spilled over the chair's curved back.

As Kier's shadow eked closer, his heart thrummed in his chest.

The chair stopped rocking.

Turning her face, the woman's profile met the sunlight.

Kier jerked away from the door, yanking his shadow back to him. He gaped at the keyhole.

There was a woman locked inside. A woman with pale skin and familiar eyes—the same intense dark-gray hue Kier had been seeing in the mirror all his life.

It wasn't possible.

An eye winked at him through the lock, and a raspy voice said, "So it's true." The words were a mix of bitterness and wonder.

He couldn't speak.

"Don't be afraid, boy." Her words bore an accent he couldn't place and the gravelly tone of a voice not often used.

"It's been fifteen years," she said. "Come closer. I want to meet my son."

The woman wore a black dress and calm expression as she inspected the shadow shaped like Kier. A shadow because Grimm had given him no key.

She was a foot shorter than him, give or take. It was hard to tell, seeing through one's mind. He studied her face. She looked younger than her voice sounded.

How often did he wonder what his mother might've looked like?

He hadn't imagined the delicate tattoos—ink that spoke of old traditions. Shaped like beads of rain, they kissed the skin beneath her eyes, trailing to her cheekbones.

Slender and pale as a ghost, this woman kept hidden was so clearly his mother it both filled Kier with gratitude and gutted him.

His uncle had told him she was dead.

While his shadow faced her inside the room, Kier sank into a crouch, pressing a hand against the door as if feeling for a heartbeat.

"I need a moment," he told her.

She's alive.

"I was just as shocked," she said, "when the Spellcaster returned after a visit with the king to tell me my only son wasn't dead. That he'd been kept not a wing away all these years. Nay," she amended. "I was boiling mad." Her expression could scathe.

The woman was a Witchist like Kier.

He could tell by the dark things she favored in the room, by the recipes and bowls and all her interests laid out on the tables. But also by the temper in her keen eyes and the abrasive way she spoke.

"Why would he keep you—" His words choked. "Why would my uncle lie?"

"'Uncle'?" she spit. "Oh, I do hope you're sitting, boy."

She went to the hearth, plucking a photo from a shelf. His shadow crept with her.

Kier frowned as the photograph appeared in his mind. Yellowed and ripped along one side as if someone had torn a third of it away, a younger woman stood in a vast marble room holding an infant.

Set on a risen dais beyond her were three thrones.

Kier's blood seemed to sing.

"My name," the woman said to him through his shadow, "is Saira Balcombe. Once, I was *viclumeni*—'bond of the gods,' as they called those wed to the rulers to propagate heirs. I was bonded to Lucius Balcombe, the very last Descendent of the Witchist god line before you arrived."

Kier couldn't move or think straight while the words and their meaning reverberated inside him.

He stayed on his knees as Saira—his mother—spoke of how Osiris Lestat had stormed the Magie palace during shifting moons, when Kier was just two. "His supporters—the first of his Royal Army—gutted the place. They left the bodies of men and women and children in pools of blood."

Kier went sheet white. *Pools of blood.*

"Some servants managed to flee." Saira's eyes were distant as she remembered, then snapped back. "Most everyone else was dead, though, and only a few taken prisoner. I was one Osiris couldn't seem to part with." She sneered. "I was barely twenty, but he took an immediate interest in me. And you."

Gutted the place.

Prisoners.

Kier had known his uncle took the kingdom during a war. But this way?

"My uncle?" He had to hear her say it. Because if it were true, if Kier was of the Witchist god line...

Saira's brow peaked. "That man is not your uncle, boy. He's no kin of yours at all." She dropped the hand holding the picture then stepped closer to Kier's shadow, hardening her eyes. "Osiris is delusional and sick with power lust. Fifteen years ago, after I refused him, he took you from me."

"Refused him?"

She cocked an eyebrow. "Refused to bed him, or to tell him what I knew about the servants and children who'd managed to escape the night of his siege. I told him I hadn't seen them go—a lie, of course, and he knew it. He was convinced survivors fled north for sanctuary and his fear and ego wouldn't let them be. He demanded I use my connections to the *volorost* there to get him into the mountains. I refused. Days later, he told me the cough you'd had was fatal and brought me your box of ashes."

Saira's gaze wandered to a small container atop a wall shelf. It wasn't laden with soot the way candles and figurines set beside it were. It had been recently polished.

"From what I gather," she continued, returning her gaze, "Osiris raised you as his blood knowing who and what you were, knowing the power he'd stolen from your father was safely trapped—away from you—inside the Witchists' primordial relic. Inside our dagger."

At that, Kier spiraled. He braced his hand on the floor, picturing the mural on his chamber ceiling. Osiris wasn't his uncle. It was a lie. It was all a lie. But why?

"At the top of those stairs, you'll find the answer to why your uncle's afraid for his throne. What he loves, and why he fears you."

The answer came. His mother.

"He wasn't just angry with you," Kier realized aloud. "He loved you, and you never loved him back."

Saira exhaled sharply through her nose. "Yes, well, I wasn't the first. His own family shunned him when they found out that his true father wasn't mortal—that his birth was the result of a Magie that'd forced himself on Osiris's mother, someone who'd served in the Magies' court. His shunning set Osiris on a warpath against Magies. He was an angry man and a petulant child, determined the magic-born would pay for his circumstances and his lack of love."

Kier felt sick.

A small part of him could understand how Osiris felt at the rejection. But the king had made certain, all these years, Kier would know the same feeling. As a means of controlling him.

He ground his fists at his side. "Did he ever hurt you?"

Saira scoffed. "He murdered my husband and told me you died. He kept me in this room since and still comes to torture me every few days with his plans for this kingdom. But I could only get him to touch me once."

"*Get* him to touch you?"

Saira paced to the corner of the room where the gray bird watched her with round eyes. She held out a hand to it.

When the bird touched her finger, it collapsed to the floor.

Kier reflexively jerked back. "What—what are you?"

Saira's brow peaked as she bent to place a hand on the bird.

It roused instantly, shaking its head, flapping back to its perch.

"With a touch, I can take or bestow breath." She straightened again, smoothed her garb, and gazed through Kier's shadow.

"But you're not a Matterist. Are you?"

Benders in the Matterist order were the only Magies Kier had ever read about who could manipulate air.

"I am Witchist," Saira replied. "But I had a very distant aunt, Messandra, who sat the Matterist throne alongside my husband and the third ruler, Kane of the Morphist line. My very small relation to Messandra bestowed me an extra affinity."

Just a drop of god magic, Kier thought, and it was power more potent than most.

When he looked at Saira, he saw absolute strength and possibility, if he could get her and Delphine out of this castle.

If he had the courage to claim the power that belonged to him and his line.

"I'm going to kill him," Kier vowed, picturing his uncle, feeling a great shift in his heart.

The chill at his wrists felt like a cold smile.

"You will someday," Saira agreed as a matter of fact. "I hope I'm there to spit on his corpse."

Kier shook his head. "Not someday. I ascend in three days. Then I'll be trained to lead his army. The Spellcaster's convinced it's the way to make things safer for our kind, from inside. But now?"

The king had killed so many. He'd lied. He'd imprisoned his mother and stolen his birthright. The simmering rage in Kier rose so vehemently, he slammed a fist against Saira's door. His knuckles cracked as the sound rang down the short, empty hall.

In Saira's room, his shadow quivered.

For a second, the woman's expression looked wary.

But Kier liked how the hatred felt. Strong.

He thought of Grimm's explanation for what Kier had done in the woods—misting, he'd called it—and it spurred an impulsive idea.

"I'll send my shadows into the king's bedchamber tonight as he sleeps," Kier said, forming plans. "I'll choke the life from him, find the key, and get you out of here."

He waited for Saira's assent. After so long, she must want out of here as badly as Kier wanted to know his mother. As much as he wanted what was his—and to never be weak again.

Saira was quiet a moment as she looked at his shadow. "The Spellcaster was right, in part. To secure true freedom, we mustn't be hasty fools. We age slowly, boy, even more slowly than the most powerful Magies—when you're centuries old, you'll still look twenty. Do you understand what I'm saying?"

"I'm starting to." And he didn't like it.

"We'll do this right. You'll need the magic of your line, but getting inside the room where Osiris keeps that dagger will require more than even your affinity. You'll need allies, for starters, a lot of them."

Through his shadow, Kier looked desperately around her room. "That will take years."

"It will. But we have something the king underestimates among his enemies. The patience and stamina to wait. To strike at the precise right time."

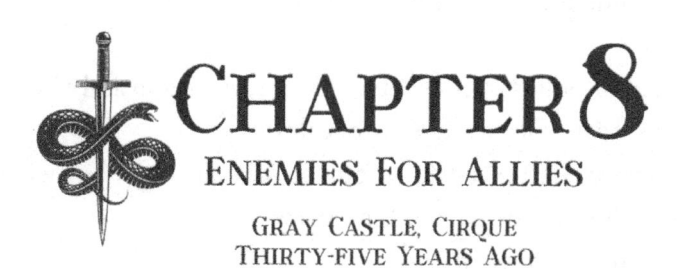

Chapter 8
Enemies For Allies
Gray Castle, Cirque
Thirty-Five Years Ago

He straightened his collar in the mirror.

"Master Kier!" Bridgen clucked through the wash room door.

Kier wanted to strangle her.

"They're here for you," she clucked again.

Kier threw open the door but kept his face calm as he strode out, doing up the last button on his new coat. It was magic-sewn for him, just for today. Stiff, with sharp angles and thick fabric. All black except for the whorls of gray thread stitched across his shoulders.

He stalked past Bridgen and shot a look at the two other servants, Gretya and Marga. He added them to the list of those who'd ever judged or wronged him.

They weren't the two Kier had wanted in his chambers on *Asenti* day.

Pausing at his chamber doors, he glanced to the mural over his bed. He thought he knew, in that moment, what god Erebus had been thinking as he smirked at the dagger on his throne chair.

The same as Kier was thinking now.

Mine.

When he pulled open the door to see Jory Dagon and a line of soldiers, Kier's face was a mask of calm.

He expected to be led downstairs to the main ballroom, where three nights ago the king held his party.

They took him south instead.

"The king's invited half of Cirque to witness your ascension," Jory told him.

Smoothing a sneer, Kier replied, "He's always liked a spectacle."

They turned a corner, and the halls rang with sounds of high-bred wealth. Shrill laughter. Clicking canes. Light boots. Snide comments.

The south wing was teeming with Crat men in gray suits, women in high fashions, and something Kier couldn't decipher: Magies in cloaks, heads bowed and trailing after Crat pairs.

As they walked corridors he'd yet to see in daylight, he memorized halls and marked exits he'd map later, once he arrived in his captain's room at the Special Army keep.

The ballroom smelled thickly of perfume and arrogance, and the crowd inside was far bigger than he'd expected.

His gaze caught immediately on Delphine, standing at the edge of the king's dais.

When Kier took his place on the dais, every person in the room watched as the *prüstrot*—the king's official testmaster—approached with a needle to begin the ceremony.

Kier was ready, in control, when a swift prick came on his wrist, delivering an injection of a pure essence that had been carefully concocted in the towers of this castle by Delphine's father.

He didn't see that man in the crowd, though.

As the *prüstrot* removed the needle from his wrist, Kier's gaze narrowed on a group of Crat boys hovering at the back of the room, until the effects of the injection overcame him. When the essence hit his blood, Kier was a fire doused with oil.

Darkness exploded from him into the room, eliciting a sudden gasp from every soul.

It was no parlor trick, this blanketing of light, but a hushed quiet, blinding the senses of everyone in the room.

How tempting it was to wrap the darkness around them all...and pull. To rid the world of Crats willing to kill Magies and a king who'd condone the murder to secure his power.

But Delphine was here, too, with several other servants, and Kier didn't trust that out of an entire crowd he would only hurt those he wanted to hurt.

He didn't trust his control.

He could imagine it, though—what he might do in that moment, if he *were* in full control.

In the darkness, his shadows would slither and sniff among the Crats and soldiers, seeking every devious smirk, every mind preening at the thought of what Kier's power, on their side, would do for their personal interests.

Those men and women would feel a chill caress their skin. They'd gasp in delight—and fright—and in the black void of this room, they'd feel that chill deepen as his dark coils slipped around their throats like constricting snakes, squeezing just enough to make their eyes water.

Kier would gather some of the darkness back into himself, enough to just glimpse the terror spreading across their faces as they realized they were about to earn the fate they'd wanted for

Magies. He would smile as those tendrils tightened, as the king grew pale in his throne chair and shook in fear, realizing every representative, every soldier, every Crat he'd beckoned here to watch Kier bend the knee, was about to lose their heads.

With his own lips upturned, Kier would flick his wrists, and his shadows would heave.

Hundreds of heads would thud against marble as bodies draped in silk or stiff in pewter wool collapsed on top of themselves, smearing the polished floor with blood.

Then Kier would turn his attention, at last, to the king. Grimm, Delphine, and all the Magies and children he'd spared, would listen to the monarch plead for his life, watch him crawl the dais until he knelt before Kier in false repentance, begging for mercy.

"Mercy," Kier would muse. "I'll give you the mercy you deserve, *Uncle*."

And the king would realize, by the arch in Kier's brow, by the way he shook his head slowly, that Kier *knew* who he truly descended from and that Kier was going to get back what belonged to him.

Looking to Delphine, he'd sneer at the king, "I'll give you the mercy you showed Rhodin."

At a clenching of Kier's fists, his shadows would crush Osiris Lestat's skull and tear him apart, piece by piece, until there was nothing left but hollow bones. And—for Saira, for Rhodin, for every Magie the king of Magus had or had yet to steal from—Kier would spit on his corpse.

The scene was so real in his mind, Kier shuddered, and a flicker of light ebbed into the ballroom, eliciting echoes of awe.

He shook with fear at himself, at how easily his dark imaginings came, at how ready his shadows were to act.

Holding the darkness in place, so that no one could see his struggle, Kier recalled Saira telling him they couldn't be hasty fools, urging him to have patience, and soon the chill inside him eased.

As he peeled back the night as the king had instructed, a round of applause erupted.

Kier clasped his hands tightly, locking his emotions behind a tight smile, as the king declared him an official ally of the crown.

"Look upon him!" Osiris called out to the room. "This allyship is the assurance of peace to come, the promise that the magic-born will settle into their place in this world! By hand of the crown, Kier and the Special Army will ensure every child has an opportunity to serve their kingdom. And with him on our side—his power at our command—we will, at last, have the sway to bring the northern region into our fold!"

As the room cheered, hungry for what the king promised, Kier saw in their faces how they craved the reassurance that their positions at the top would be safe. He saw how they valued their own wealth and prosperity over the struggle of his people.

The king had done it, then.

He'd made Kier a symbol.

Oh, he would be a symbol.

The king spoke long about plans for the academy next, to more applause. When it was over, Grimm bowed, and Kier made a show of dipping his head, too, while clasping his wrists tightly.

For the next hour, he tried to ignore the opulence and arrogance dripping from every conversation, as he was paraded around the room by Jory Dagon.

This was the second part—the commander of the mortal army giving his endorsement, introducing the new Special Army leader to every Crat in the room.

"Let them see you," the king had said. "Assure them."

Some kept a wide berth, smiling nervously, preferring to hold to their drinks rather than shake Kier's hand.

It didn't scathe anymore, he found. He was nourished by their fear of him. Though his head did pound with the noise of clinking glasses and oblivious laughter.

At a table laden with food, Jory clasped a man's wide shoulder.

When the bear of a man turned, red and sweaty from drink and from being stuffed into a suit, he bore such a striking resemblance to his daughter, Kier nearly lunged at him—an impulse he'd have to work on—as he heard Nisha in his head: *My father says every Magie should be hunted and put in chains for the centuries you sat the throne and led us into sin.*

"Brigham," Jory greeted.

"Dagon!" the man bellowed in greeting, clapping his hand on Jory's back. "I had my doubts, when Representative Coyle told me of the king's plans last evening. But... With what's happened to my Nisha... Frankly, we could use an insider to put the rest of them in their place."

The man's expression tightened as he noticed Kier.

It would always be that way. Every person Kier met would look at him and see the creature he was, lurking beneath Kier's measured façade.

It was a sacrifice he could live with, for now.

"Yes, of course," Jory agreed. "May I officially introduce you to the new Captain of the Special Army? You'll find Kier is highly motivated to see that achieved."

"I should hope so," the man replied. "It's a far superior future than the alternative."

A threat.

"Sir." Kier nodded. "I was sorry to hear of your daughter. How terrible to lose someone so...precious."

Brigham's eyes bounced to Kier, then quickly back to Jory. He was nervous.

Kier smiled.

"Yes," the man said tightly. "At least the heathen was brought to justice."

Kier kept his face neutral, though his shadows quivered at his wrist. He clamped them down.

He knew the despicable story Jory and the king had concocted. Rhodin, a servant boy, had gone wandering in the woods. He'd stalked the hunters and used his affinity. He'd paid for it.

"Well," Brigham said. "You should meet the rest of my family. It's always inspiring, isn't it? To know who you're fighting for."

Kier saw Delphine's face in his mind, and his eyes flicked in a moment of weakness to the door, where she was taking an empty glass from a representative. Already, she looked thinner.

Who had she been assigned to?

Brigham stepped aside, and a boy stepped forward. "One of my sons," the man introduced.

Kier froze, eyes locked on a familiar red handkerchief the boy was using to wipe his forehead. He was tall, lanky, and his eyes shone in recognition for the briefest moment before he recovered and said to Kier, "It was sure darker than I thought it'd be."

Kier's mind spun to the woods. To this boy, nervous on his steed.

"Darker than I thought it'd be."

"It's not so bad... Your eyes will adjust. And near the lake, the canopy opens."

"I mean," the boy added, snapping Kier's attention back, "the whole room was just engulfed in it."

"Don't mind Vesh," Brigham said. "Never got over his childish fears of the dark."

The boy bristled but laughed it off quickly, sticking his hand out to Kier. "Vesh Derringer. Why don't I introduce you to my cousins?"

Reluctantly, Jory nodded at Kier before letting himself be swept into conversation with Brigham about a crown policy to make indentures legal. "Think of the clear message it would send to the heathens. It's been fifteen years since the war. The army, the academy, indentures—it's time we hit them with a hammer."

"I'll bring it to the king," Jory replied as the two wandered off.

Kier's gaze scorched their backs. But the boy—Vesh—wagged his head. "This way."

Kier bit his lip, following him to the back of the room near the tapestries, where two other young hunters sat waiting.

He knew what to say.

The king and his advisers had prepared Kier a story. The hunt had been a test to see if Crats and loyal Magies could work side by side. Kier, the king spun it, had been gravely injured by that rebellious little servant and tried to save the others before crawling his way out of the woods to go for help, ahead of the other boys.

The two stood to greet Kier.

He recognized the smaller of them as the one in the group who'd hung back with the hounds. It was the second one, who'd kept his hat tipped and a hand on his hunting gun, who stepped forward.

He leered appreciatively at Kier. "Kercher. Wyatt Kercher. And if I'd known what you were, whew!" He smirked. "I would've insisted you hunt with our team."

Kier's stoic brows knitted, but he bit back a reply as two boisterous Crats passed by their huddle—*"Enslave them all, that's what I say..."*

Kier fisted his hands at his sides, taking a breath. "You're not upset?" he asked the three of them. "That I couldn't help your friends?"

Vesh, on Kier's left, lowered his head, glancing around. "We know what really happened out there."

From his pocket, Vesh retrieved something silver. A ring, Kier realized with dread. The boy rotated it between two fingers so Kier could see a crown forged in the metal.

Nisha's father had been wearing one just like it, as were half the Crats in this room. Only, the crown emblem on this one had been blackened by heat. Or something else.

Before Kier could defend himself, Vesh stretched out his hand to offer him the ring, nodding for Kier to take it, then shocked Kier by saying quietly, "Nisha and Sorin were as obsessed as my father with punishing your people. My sister—my *stepsister*, I mean—well, she liked to torture animals." Vesh swallowed, his sad eyes lifting to meet Kier's. "She liked to torture me, too."

Kercher nodded his agreement. "Maybe Ahren wasn't awful on his own—spineless, for sure, and heading a bad way, how he idolized Nisha—but there aren't many who'll mourn the other two. That's just the truth."

Kier inspected the third boy, though, who remained silent.

Vesh followed Kier's gaze. "That's Arkimen. It's not you he's uncomfortable with. He just prefers the company of animals to parties."

Over Vesh's shoulder, Kier caught sight of Jory heading their way.

"What do you want?" he said quietly to the three. They had information on Kier. They'd made that known. Despite their politeness, despite despising Nisha, they wanted something. But nothing could get in Kier's way now.

Nothing.

"We each have a pile of wealth coming our way when our fathers pass," said Vesh, raising a brow in a way that suggested the time couldn't come soon enough.

"And?"

Kercher rocked on his boots. "And we'd like to expand our riches, but not by enslaving a bunch of Magies. There's far more fun we could have...together."

Vesh stuffed his hands in his coat pockets. "I've heard the vile things they're planning in Cirque, and I know what you can do. We're not looking to fund a *war*"—he whispered the word—"but if you find yourself in a position to steer a different course, you can consider us allies."

Allies. On the inside.

He slid Nisha's ring onto his right hand and nodded at the three boys as Jory approached. "Your king will appreciate your loyalty." Kier bowed a farewell, and as Jory steered him away, the word *king* echoed in his mind.

He hadn't meant Osiris Lestat.

Leaning in, Jory said, "The carriages are being brought around."

"What about what I asked for?" Kier's heart thumped in anticipation.

"You did well today," Jory replied as they left the ballroom. "The king is granting you five minutes."

J ory led him down another set of unfamiliar halls.

Kier elaborated on the map he'd begun charting earlier.

As they rounded a corner, he saw two Crat guests in suits who'd strayed from the festivities. They were approaching a set of iron doors where four soldiers stood straight as arrows, armed with guns.

Beside him, Jory stiffened, cursing.

A rush of feet came behind him and Kier, two servants hurrying past them up the hall. As the servants reached the guests, one said, "Sirs. Our apologies, but this hall is strictly off-limits. Please, come along."

Meandering back toward the ballroom, the guests' heads bent together and, as they passed, Kier caught their whispers: "...Magie relics."

He nearly threw Jory out of his way and unleashed his shadows right there.

He sensed the rumor was true immediately, though Jory quickly led him on. Like a magnet to metal, Kier's bones ached for it, so close. It felt like need.

"Keep up," Jory commanded. "Your carriage leaves shortly."

Patience.

His blood still singing, his shadows discontent, he followed down a maze of more halls. They were nearing the front entrance to the castle when Jory opened a door that led into a small study.

What Kier was greeted with—a girl in a red dress, standing at the window overlooking the front yard—was another sort of need. This one he knew well.

"Five minutes," Jory reminded, then shut the door as he left.

Her hair was fixed tightly in a crown of braids. Her hands twitched where she hugged herself. She didn't turn.

He stepped beside her. "Delphine."

"Kier," she choked, finally looking at him, and he registered her darkly rimmed eyes and sallow skin.

A swift chill swept through him, and his chest heaved in angry breaths. "What's he done?"

It'd only been a few days, and she looked deeply unwell.

"Shouldn't you be celebrating?" she asked, venom in her voice.

Kier flinched at her tone. "I had to see you before I left. I had to know you were safe."

She turned back to the window. "Well, now you've seen me."

"Where do they have you? Serving the representatives?"

She laughed, but it no longer sounded like her laughter. It was too flat. Devoid of humor. "Didn't your uncle tell you?" She turned to face him. "He's made me one of his personal attendants."

Kier became ice—stiff, cold, hard. "I won't let him hurt you. I—I'll do everything I can to make certain—"

"You'll do nothing, Kier. You did nothing." Her implication was a slap, a reference to Rhodin.

She didn't understand, then. "I couldn't lose you. I had to keep him from killing you."

"You should've let him."

"Delphine," he hissed.

"You stopped the Crats in the woods. You could've stopped the king."

Kier was forced a full step back, her eyes were so fierce. Clearly, she blamed him for Rhodin. Just as he blamed himself.

But her ferocity fizzled as she bit her lip and shook her head as if to clear her anger. It was unnerving how placid and smooth her face became.

He reached for her. He couldn't help it. He took her arms tightly and forced her to look at him. Glancing quickly to the door and back, he swore, "I will stop him."

She did the same, her gaze flitting beyond him a moment, and she seemed to realize what he was confessing.

"Don't tell me what you're planning," she whispered.

His mouth closed, and he realized he'd been about to. He shouldn't. Saira said to tell no one, not even Grimm Hermes, how exactly they planned to undo the king in the years to come.

"Do you love me?" he asked instead.

She frowned. "You can't just ask a girl outright like that."

He released a tight breath and pulled her into his chest. "It has to look like this is over," he whispered. "He'd only use you against me."

She stiffened in his arms.

"It'll take time, but I'll come for you. My heart... It will never change."

She shivered, but when Kier pulled away, he didn't see the desire he felt himself. Her eyes, instead, were empty.

Good. He hoped she could keep up the act whenever his name was mentioned.

Stepping out of his hold, she turned to the window and said, her words clipped and tight, "Good luck at the army, Master Kier."

But as Jory returned to take him and they left the room, he swore he heard her whisper, "Happy birthday."

They crossed the Rott River and traversed the cliff hills by carriage, a convoy of coaches and other wagons at the rear.

Torch lights greeted them at a formidable gate, where Kier saw a pair of Fabricaters with hands on a stone sign, forging the last letter to read: *HIS MAJESTY'S SPECIAL ARMY.*

No, Kier thought. *My army.*

So long as he earned that support at *Asenti,* the king had agreed he'd be no grunt here. And it'd been clear to everyone in that room. Kier was more powerful than any Magie they'd met, apart from Grimm maybe, for now.

"I'll learn on the job, with your guidance," he'd told the king at their final dinner the evening before. He'd spent the entire hour making himself appear the obedient nephew he'd been just days ago. "I'll do as you would."

Lying had come surprisingly easy. Then again, Delphine had taught him what he could do with practice.

The king had liked Kier's change of heart.

He mounted the keep stairs, turning to observe the army's first recruits as they stepped out from wagons and carriages.

They were all Magies, each one. His kind. But he wouldn't be naïve enough to assume that just because they all bore magic it meant they wanted what Kier did. He would test them, each one, in the years to come.

He inspected them, young men and women, dismissing the ones who stared reverently at him and memorizing the faces of those who clenched their fists while glaring at the massive stone keep.

Those were the ones he needed in his circle. The ones hungry for revenge.

Chapter 9
The Dark King
Spellcaster Hamlet, Wythe
Present Day

When Darkness returns, he feels resurrected.

Amid the raining debris of battle and Jasper Salt's fervent shouts, the Darkwielder bolts upright as power seethes again beneath his skin—the power of the god within him.

Ophelia Dannan scattered his darkness quite far. But these shadows are too ancient and too strong to be destroyed, not as long as he's alive to wield them.

It's nothing now to press them into his wounds and staunch the bleeding, nothing to make a band of the thick tendrils to carry him out of this pit.

As they lift him up, his mind tries to wander back to memories of Delphine and what happened between the day he was sent to lead the Special Army and the night, fifteen years ago now, when he failed in his first attempt to retrieve her and the dagger. The same night he fled from Gray Castle with Saira and a young boy at his side—but not Delphine. And not the dagger, which he recovered only recently.

But those memories are better left buried.

The Darkwielder snuffs his past as if it were a lamplight, and he rises above the seam. There, he's met with a gust of frigid air, Jasper Salt, and the aftermath of Ophelia's destruction: a crumpled dais, billowing smoke, bodies, and the chasm splitting the ground. It snakes like a vast, empty river straight through the Spellcaster temple and a forest grove beyond Wythe, then farther, as far as his gaze can reach.

Gasps and coughs draw his attention to the knoll.

Amid the smoke, silhouettes slowly step forward. Then more, and more. Hundreds more.

When they see him, the rebel soldiers fall to their knees one by one, wolves bowing to their pack leader. His determination swells at the sight of these Special Army soldiers who were recruited by Jasper Salt, as Captain Rivmere, all of whom are now loyal to his fight against the crown.

Jasper comes around to face him, obscuring his view. His proxy's burnished eyes are wide with moisture from the whipping wind and emotion as he sinks to the sod and bows his head. When his face lifts again, he's not the arrogant Rivmere, but the young boy with violence in his eyes and revenge in his soul—the one the Darkwielder took with him that night from Gray Castle fifteen years ago.

The Darkwielder rakes his eyes over the soldiers, who each bear the mark of their loyalty—the mark of Darkness—on their skin. Their faces are marred with dirt and, while the Darkwielder has grown used to cold things, these men and women tremble in the bitter wind.

Jasper stands, shoulders shrugging up to protect his ears in his collar, and follows the Darkwielder's gaze. "They'll fight for you. Whatever you command of them next, they'll do."

"I know." But they're replete. Exhausted. Some are in need of a healer.

The Darkwielder turns to survey the camp behind them, where half the tents that have been set afire still smolder.

Quietly, he asks, "And the bastard king?"

Jasper's brows pinch. "Escaped."

Escaped.

As he thought. And with weapons as powerful, perhaps more so in their vast numbers, than even the magic the Darkwielder's Special Army possesses.

He fists his hands at his side so tightly that the black crown ring bites into his palm, and he relishes the pain, the reminder.

He's no longer weak.

He is…

"Someday they will call you king," Saira assured him after they'd escaped the castle and stopped to water their stolen steeds in the valley along the Black Silt River. They'd been riding for hours and he was certain he'd never shake the sting of failing to retrieve the Dark Shadow Dagger.

Nearly twenty years it had taken for the time to be right and not only had he failed, but he'd gotten most of his men killed.

He hung his head while the boy sat quietly on his horse. "I'm nothing now," he told her.

Saira's curtain of dark hair veiled an eye as she lowered the hood of her cloak. "Kier Lestat is dead," she told him, no trace of mourning in her words. "Don't dwell on his losses. We're alive to fight again." She tipped up her chin. "Choose another name, one that announces who you are."

But he was nothing after everything he'd lost that night. Staring blankly at the dark water, he asked, "What did you call me when I was born?"

A natural shadow crossed her face. "You used to crawl into your father's sanctum at the palace. Amid bones and arcane books and dead things he'd bottled on shelves. Less than a year old and drawn to your father's fascinations, wanting to play with the darkness."

"A darkwielder," he mused, filled with a sense of awe.

Saira aimed a troubled look at him. "Be careful, boy. If Osiris hadn't murdered your father, there were other things—his own proclivities—that may eventually have done it. Take care you don't embrace your darkness too fully the way he did."

The Darkwielder loosens his fists.

His mother's words were wise, perhaps. But the woman's always been full of warnings. And as he surveys his shivering soldiers and the great seam now stretching through Magus, he realizes that he's not defeated at all.

Eking out shadow, he commands it high above the knoll to show him what stretches on either side of the chasm. Ophelia Dannan has left him a gift—an idea and a means to make a bigger sanctuary of this kingdom, a way to finally start taking it back.

Yes, they will call him king.

And Ophelia would make a fine queen, he realizes, remembering the feeling of warmth in her presence, the inviting light inside her, beckoning to a part of him that hadn't felt anything in a long while.

Facing the seam with a smile, he lets his boots slide to the edge, feeling far steadier now than he did when he lay in the chasm.

Fifteen years ago, after that failed siege, he rose a mountain to make a small refuge for those who wouldn't bend to the crown, where magic could be free. The Belly has grown since then, under care of Vesh and his so-called allies running things. Crowded, it also grew wilder, with the Darkwielder hidden in shadows while Jasper, as Rivmere, worked on turning half the Special Army to lay one last siege.

The siege that cursed the king and brought Ophelia Dannan home to Magus.

Jasper shifts restlessly at his side, waiting for the Darkwielder's instruction.

He made a mountain without the Dark Shadow. What might he do with it?

"We'll be needing more soldiers to finish this war," the Darkwielder says as the wind howls through his mantle and he stares into the bowels of the chasm. "And a larger sanctuary."

"What's your plan?" Jasper asks.

For a moment, the Darkwielder's gaze flicks up to where he watched an onslaught of Royal Army soldiers eaten by waves of his dark mist. So well-practiced was he in wielding it now, he left *nothing* behind. No skein of flesh, no bone or ash, no evidence at all apart from footprints in the snow.

"For starters," he replies, "we take the west."

He raises his arms, and Jasper instinctively folds back into the throng of soldiers still on bended knee. His audience watches intently as the wielder calls Darkness from his bones.

A mass of it clings to his back—like dark wings—and a smirk lifts his lips. His power gathers quick as lightning, pulling every speck of the night inside of it—growing it—until he is a vast, infinite storm of vengeance.

Mine, he thinks as he hurls it from himself into the gaping chasm, filling the hollow earth with a viscous, violent Darkness that's thirsty for revenge.

It's not a wave of mist this time. Not a pack of shadows. It is instead an impassable, dark river of snapping jaws and teeth and claws. His dark monsters.

He fills it so full of them that any soul who dares cross it might never escape.

The black river rages, cracking and lengthening the chasm as it bites through the ground, north to south.

And when he's finished, his river has cleaved the kingdom in two. The monarchy stands in the east, cut off from the Darkwielder's new west. So his people will truly be free.

So that his enemies will see his power and know he's coming.

*The story continues in Every Thread of Light,
book two of the Whispers of Dust & Darkness series.*

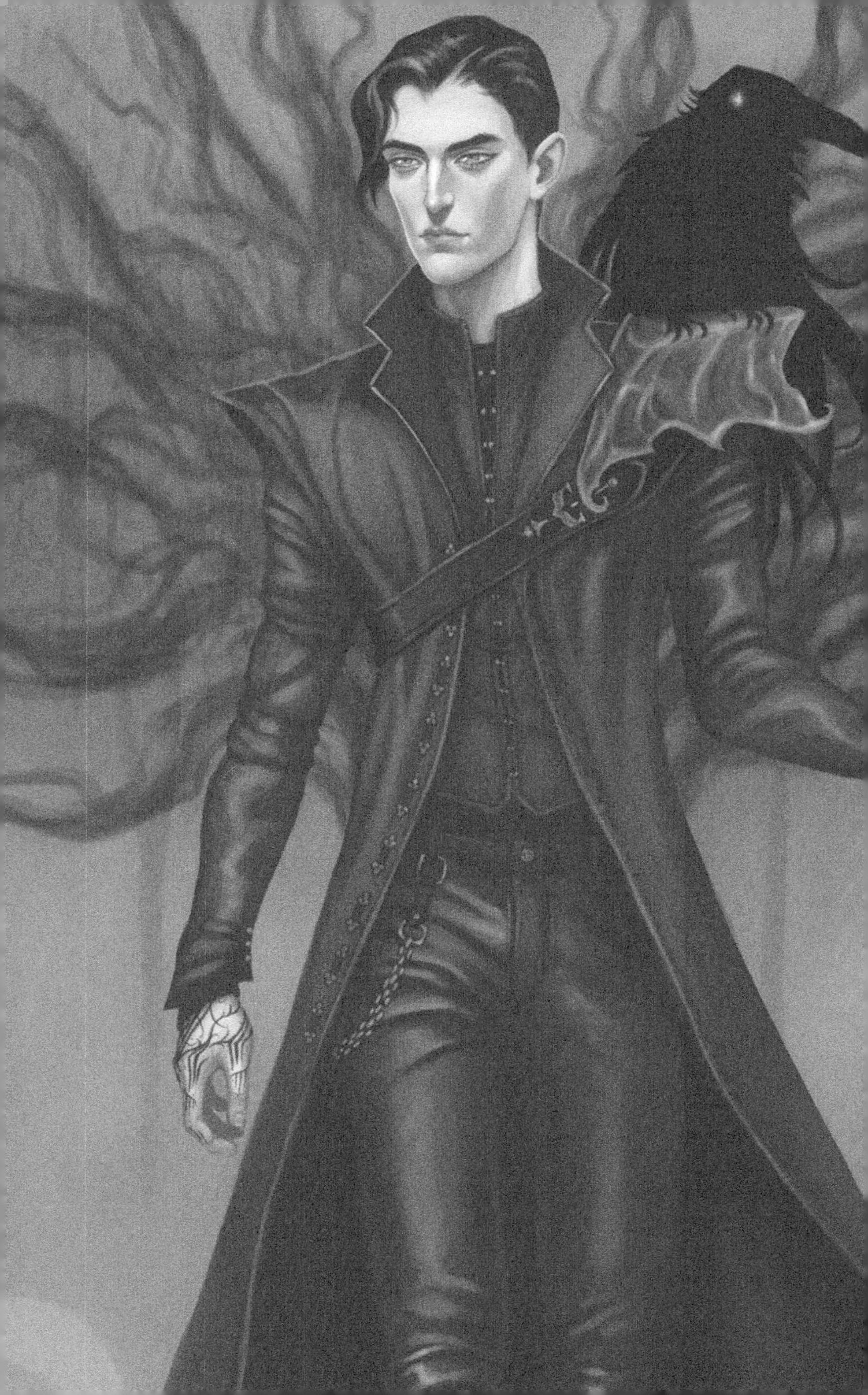

THE STORY CONTINUES...

KEEP READING FOR AN EXCERPT.

CHAPTER 1
Alive & Unwell
The Underbelly, Kingdom of Magus
1st Day in the New Winter
Ophelia is with Falcon

Ophelia Dannan wanted to be done with hiding. No more resets. No more stories. Yet, under a dangerous midnight sky glittering with winter, magic, and the anticipation of war, it seems she's the fugitive once more.

High above the streets of the Underbelly, she studies the reckless gap between rooftops sprawling before her and, with a muttered prayer to the goddess Selene, flings herself into the frigid winter wind as if she bore wings.

She lands on a knee beside a rough-shaven smuggler, her a ravaged ship come to shore, Falcon Thames a tower of vigilance.

Something stirs in her chest—a flutter—when he perks a brow and offers her a warm hand up. His fingers slip from hers to graze the lightblade in his baldric as they approach the roof wall. "Not far now," he notes, tucking his chin into the high collar of his coat.

"Good." Gods willing, reconnecting with an ally will put them one move closer to freedom.

Ophelia has felt the anticipation of seeing the Spellcaster for hours since leaving Rook, ever since Trix's summons came as jolting as winter's fall on Magus. A winter, and summons, as unexpected as the silence sprawling through the city of pleasure six stories below now.

In the middle of night with snow burying the streets, wind dragging its sharp claws across her skin, the Belly—the Darkwielder's sanctuary—should pulse like a wild, beating heart. There should be Crats, basking in drunken debauchery, especially here in Ravish.

"It's too quiet," she mutters, unease an unwanted passenger as she surveys the scene, feeling the need to triple check they left no trace to be followed.

Falcon nods, as if between the pricking snow and curtains of magic that cloak the night he can feel it, too.

"Let's go," she says. Her hands numbing at the fingers, she starts to rise just as the wind carries a scream that could cut the cold.

A man in a gray coat barrels up the street with the fear of the gods in his gait, chased by a dark streak nipping viciously at his heels. With a lurch in her chest, Ophelia realizes it's a shadow at the same moment Falcon curses.

Gripping the edge of the roof, she sees the man veer and shuffle on the ice. He collides with the façade of a derelict apartment door that's rotting at the hinges. "No," he moans. "No!"

An unfamiliar figure in dark clothes steps under a gas lamp, into its snow-dusted glow, his silhouette carved with sharp edges. A Shadowcaster. "Crat," he spits like a curse. "You've been coming into our city like you own it, but that's all changing now, isn't it?"

Ophelia starts to her feet, magic humming inside, but Falcon clasps her arm. "This is the Belly, Teacup. We can't be seen."

The man lets out a wailing cry as the shadows lunge. With a crack, the Crat's cry cuts like the scratch of a song and the man folds to a heap.

Her nails bite the brick of the roof as the shadows rip back to their caster.

She has lived in danger her whole life. Run from it. Slept in its midst. More recently, faced it head on. But Falcon is right about the Belly. There's nothing safe or friendly about the city that's harbored magic like an incubator. Especially now, with news of the revolution spreading.

Waiting for the street to clear, she fills her lungs with a shock of winter air and the stench of Ravish—that reek of petrol, perfume, and wet stone. The scent of danger.

Lifting her gaze to the sheens of dust that dip and dive in the night, her senses come alive—alert—amidst magic that has no master.

It's a reminder of what they fight for.

Freedom.

Four bells faintly chime in succession across the city.

"Dawn's coming," Falcon notes. "We need to be off the streets." He pats a hand on the wall, looking through his lashes at her. "Ladies first?"

She snorts. "When have you ever called me 'lady'?"

With his chuckle echoing and the cold nipping, she alights down the rails along the length of the stone façade, her woolen dress and fur cloak billowing. Her satchel, hastily packed before they left Rook, jostles at her hip when she slips to the street.

She doesn't look at the dead Crat.

Keeping heads down, they traverse in silence the rest of the way to Ravish, the Belly's eastern-most territory. As is habit, she memorizes the route, drawing a map in her mind of the mazing alleys, the trinket and smoke shops, the canals where boatmen sleep under thick wools in tied-off dinghies.

When they reach a hotel bricked black and trimmed in gold, she scours the natural shadows, nearly missing the woman on the corner with her arms crossed over a thick coat and trousers belted at the waist to hug her petite frame.

"About time," Trix calls, pushing off the lamppost where she's been waiting.

Ophelia's struck by how changed she looks—not just all the leather she wears, but the hard edge in her eyes. She wastes no time pulling the Spellcaster into a hug, but almost right away feels Trix stiffen in the embrace, as if uncomfortable with the display.

Pulling back, Ophelia swipes at a rogue tear that's slipped to her cheek. "Sorry, I'm just relieved you're alive."

With a rueful smile, Trix shakes her head. "What did I tell you about apologizing?"

Women are always doing that.

But Ophelia's own smile weakens at the sight of the taut lines etching Trix's face. Evidence she's been bracing against pain, hardening herself.

Memories of Trix's twin, Cleo, barrage Ophelia like a battering of snowflakes, pushing a lump into her throat. Trix must blame her. Getting involved with Ophelia got her sister murdered.

"Wick Sneed," Ophelia starts, and just his name stirs a spark of fury. "He didn't hurt you?"

Trix casts a look down the street as though she half-expects to see him there, sneering in the murk of the budding morning. "I didn't catch up with him."

"I can't believe you went after him. That was—"

"Goddamn stupid," Falcon cuts from where he's been watching their reunion. Stepping onto the curb, he combs the Spellcaster over, a smirk coloring his lips. "Trix Farrow. Seems you've got as many lives as you had cats once."

Trix stares with mock loathing at him, as she always has. It's a relief, actually. A flicker of the woman Ophelia began to call a friend. Setting off toward the hotel, she calls, "Unless you two enjoy this bloody weather, follow me."

Ophelia was expecting a place they could lie low and recalibrate, not heavily weaponed Magies guarding the front doors of a hotel.

After passing through an old-world foyer dotted with crystal chandeliers, she runs eyes over faded-gold wallpaper in a long hall strewn with tasseled rugs, dark wood paneling, and polished sconces. Décor that's a nod to a more prosperous city—maybe a city that was safe once—before the Belly became somewhere magic-born hide.

Trudging beside Trix up a curving staircase and down a narrow hall, Ophelia counts twenty more Magies who look like they've seen plenty of fights. The men and women are well-muscled. Some of their noses are bent, and many bear scars on their brows or hands. Each wears an assortment of colored leather and wool, and an array of weapons stuffed wherever they could find a sheath.

They stop sorting through food and medical supplies, their gazes lifting to follow her.

Once upon a time, her mother taught her to run, but Ophelia has since taught herself not to cower. She stares back at the

Magies, surprised to feel Falcon's hand hover at the small of her back.

He leans to catch Trix's eye and lifts a brow. "This place was full of Crat guests a few weeks ago."

Noting his protective hand, Trix shrugs. "Things change. We'll be using it as a base now for a citizen's militia."

Falcon huffs. "Right. When Wyatt Kercher finds out you seized his hotel, his dogs will just give up the bone."

"He won't be a problem," she assures as they round another hall. "We've already started recruiting Magies who want to learn combat."

Ophelia cuts a glance at her in surprise. "That was fast. The war just started."

"Did it?" Trix asks. Sconce light flickers over her serious features as they approach the end of the hall where she gestures ahead to a set of double doors. "Ophelia, you can take the suite." She flicks a hand toward an adjacent door as they near it. "This one's open for you, smugger."

Ophelia tenses. She doesn't want to admit how much she wants Falcon to stay, not in front of Trix, but the idea of being alone with her memories is suffocating. To her relief, he walks straight past the offered room without a word, striding toward her suite.

With irritation simmering in her eyes, Trix follows, her mouth clamped shut.

Their mutual annoyance and sniping are oddly comforting. The two act like siblings, and it reminds her of how it was sometimes growing up with Hart.

In the suite, Falcon drops their satchels on the bed. His eyes crawl the gold- and red-papered walls, drapes, and fine furnishings before they narrow back toward the hall of Magies. "Can't say 'combat leader' doesn't suit you—I've seen you fight—but who the hell are your friends?" he asks Trix. "I don't recognize them."

The Spellcaster leans casually against the door frame. "You don't recognize them because you've been...gone." Her gaze drops to the floor, a small acknowledgment of the horrors they relayed to her via summons earlier, about what happened in Wythe and why they're here, two people short.

Don't think about it now.

"The Magies here are newly free," Trix explains. "They didn't all get a chance to prove themselves, what with the arena closed, but they're out of their indentures and hungry for vengeance. They're good fighters."

Falcon's brows knit. "The fights are shut down?" *Barbaric fights*, from how he's described them. Crats throwing their Magies into pits, waging bets, forcing them to tear one another down for a chance to earn their freedom.

"They stopped about a week ago," Trix says. "And don't worry about my friends. They're on the right side."

Side.

Magies versus the monarchy, Ophelia considers with a quiet little simmer of wrath in her chest. *One side fighting for freedom, one to keep control. And what is each willing to become to win?*

While Falcon busies himself prowling the suite, inspecting every tapestry and closet—even the bolt on the balcony door—Ophelia settles at the wall beside Trix. From the corner of her eye, she studies the woman's sharper edges, the lack of usual color in her wardrobe, the baldric she has slung across her shoulder that's replaced her spellbag in favor of blades.

Ophelia could drown in guilt. Maybe Trix is a woman who makes her own choices, but Ophelia's at least partly to blame for the caster's circumstance and all she sacrificed when she followed them to Magus.

She steals her friend's eye. "I'm sorry about your sister. I know that's not enough, but are you"—she swallows—"are you truly okay?"

Trix's face is a mask as she chews a lip and studies the floorboards. "I will be."

Ophelia touches her arm. "It was brave how you went after Sneed."

"It was reckless."

"What happened after you passaged here?"

Trix glances to where Ophelia's hand rests. "I found a purpose." Stepping out of reach with a smile that doesn't quite light her eyes, she backs through the door. "You two look like something my cats coughed up. Get some sleep."

Night explodes inside a dream.

The ground clefts, shaking and trembling as guns and magic spark. In the throes of battle, Wythe's great temple burns and screams ring from children trapped inside it.

Death is everywhere.

The king is escaping.

And the darkness inside Ophelia, drawn from the Gray King, is a river of ice that settles so comfortably in her bones she might believe she was born of shadows instead of light.

"Kill him, Ophelia!" The Darkwielder's plea cuts across the dais to her.

Catching sight of him hanging in a chasm, she goes still as stone. His power, a tether between them, resounds in her, calling her to act.

Beyond a doubt, she knows what he wants her to do—kill the king and catalyze the revolution. But this a nightmare and she knows what's to come instead.

The Darkwielder will fall and lose control of the shadows that spin like a hurricane around the Spellcaster hamlet. The darkness will waterfall and beasts will spring up to claw men, women, and children to ribbons. And when it happens, Ophelia will face an impossible choice—extinguish the king's life or vanquish the shadows to save the innocents. There won't be time to do both.

As the Darkwielder loses his grip and shadows spring, her decision plays out.

The tingle of *maether* gathers in the golden ridges of her arm as she teeters on the edge of a command. Then she sees herself, standing on that broken dais, looking nothing like the girl who hid in the mortal world for four years in fear. She is a woman with hair as wild as her mother's and dark eyes threaded with golden light—a goddess incarnate.

In that split second, she wonders if there might be a way, after all, to do both: save the innocents and free herself from the king.

In the nightmare, her hands rise to press firmly against her chest as she takes a single, determined breath, imagining a different ending to the battle of Wythe, and thinks, *Destroy us.*

A thousand suns explode through the dream.

To her panic—and relief—light tunnels from her arm to the ground and missiles straight into the abyss, seeking the Darkwielder before shattering her own heart...

Ophelia bolts with a cry in bed, clawing at her chest. In a fury of shoving covers away, her foot snags on the sheets and, with her heart slamming against her ribs, she slides onto the hard floor, smacking her knees upon the wood.

Panting, she realizes where she is—when she is.

It's just the hotel.

Vaguely, she registers the low dimness of the room hugging darkened shapes of furniture. She's slept the whole day, and the evening has set.

Pushing to her feet against a wave of adrenaline, she searches for the reassuring outline of Falcon in bed, but he's not there.

The nightmare presses in.

Panic climbs the rungs of her chest, up her throat, and sends her scrambling toward the wash room.

She doesn't make it to the toilet.

Ophelia's eyes water as she retches into a porcelain tub, hands gripping the edge of the clawfoot where she kneels on the cold tiles. With a cheek resting against the edge, she fights for control of her breath and notices a glow pulsing into the narrow room from a small square window.

Outside, particles shiver against the glass, making little pings. When they have her attention, a deluge of soft whispers fills her throbbing head, warbling over top of one another, as nonsensical as ever.

Her head aches, and aches, and in her mind, she sees blood. Grimm's blood, before his body disintegrated and became *dust*. It still doesn't make sense. Why would he become particles when other magic-born die and become ash?

The whispers breathe louder—like bees.

"Leave me alone," she rasps. Maybe it's selfish, but in this dark moment, she can't bear the light.

A prattle comes again, the dust vibrating like shaken stars, pressing itself closer against the pane as if to see her better or be let inside.

"Go away," she wills, clenching her stomach. Yet it whorls in protest, like she's asked it to do the impossible. Picking her head up, she begs, *"Please."*

The shimmers of light scatter like an unkindness of daws, taking the glow and whispers, leaving her head mercifully silent.

Clinging to the tub, waiting for her tremors to ease, she tries to gate against the lingering snatches of her nightmare. But this is it—everything that's happened catching up. Rune's vacant eyes as he stabbed a pick-blade into Grimm's chest. Falcon and Hart being beaten with the butts of soldiers' guns. The feel of Hart's hand slipping out of hers before they all jumped for the passage. Only two of them making it through.

With a bare arm, she wipes a tear off her cheek and releases her grip on the tub to draw her legs into herself.

I am Ophelia Dannan, the daughter of Elora, the direct descendant of Selene, the goddess of light and protection. I am of the dust, the breath of life. I am stronger than my darkest hour, and I will not break. Whatever I must do, I will free this kingdom.

She recites the words again.

And again.

But alone in the dark, experiencing echoes of what they lost and left behind, she can't feel the conviction of the words. Can't forget she let the King of Magus live and failed to save Grimm Hermes. Failed to keep them all together.

Beyond the wash room, a door rattles and clicks.

Dragged from her thoughts by the sharpening awareness that someone has entered their suite, Ophelia scrabbles to her feet and snatches the blade sheathed at her thigh.

About the Author

Sarah Zimm discovered at age six she could climb a high maple carrying a blank notebook. She's been writing ever since. Sarah lives in the Midwest with her husband, son, and shadow-chasing mutt. *Every Dark Shadow* is her debut fantasy novel. You can find her online at @AuthorSarahZimm.